summer NIGHTS

A Novella Duo

Push It Forward &

Hold Your Horses

(Blythe College 2.5)

ROCHELLE PAIGE

Editing by Mickey Reed
Cover by Melissa Gill of MG Book Covers & Designs
Formatting by Champagne Formats

Champagne
Formats

ISBN-10: 1500317977
ISBN-13: 978-1500317973

Books by Rochelle Paige

Blythe College Series

PUSh the ENVELOPE
Hit the WALL

Dedication

Crystal, Harper, Ella, Tessa & Kristi –

Your friendship & support means the world to me. Although I'm pretty sure my world would explode if a day went by without chatting with y'all. What would I do for giggles? And where would I find stuff to drool over? Smooches!!!

PUSH it FORWARD

by ROCHELLE PAIGE

Chapter 1

Drake

"HOLD STILL," I growled as I gripped Alexa's hips and thrust into her from behind. She continued to wiggle her ass, trying to move back so I'd hit her just right, but I wasn't ready for her to come yet. I wanted it to build more before I let her go over the edge.

"Drake, please," she begged.

I leaned over, forcing her chest further into the bed and bit down into her shoulder. "Not yet, baby. You'll get there, but hold on just a little bit longer for me."

"Mmmmm," she murmured as she settled at my words. "Promise?"

I groaned deep in my throat at the sound of her throaty voice. I ran my hands from her ass and up her back until I gripped her shoulders. "Fuck yeah," I swore as I slammed inside.

Her hands reached out to grip the sheets as she struggled not to move. I could feel her clenching against my cock each time I pulled out of her body. I slowed my movements until each slide was painstakingly slow. I could already feel the telltale tingle in my balls, and I didn't know if I could even hold on any longer but I had to try. I spread her legs open further so I could get deeper.

"Oh, God," she cried out as I slid all the way back in and rotated my hips to grind against her.

"I want you to feel me like this for days. If I'm going to be away from you for so long, then you can be damned sure I will make you remember who this pussy belongs to, baby," I murmured into her ear.

My words sent her over the edge and I desperately tried to hold back as she shuddered underneath me. I held still, my cock buried inside until she started to calm underneath me and then I pulled out so I could flip her over. "Wrap your legs around me," I ordered as I drove back in, surging hard and deep as I jack-hammered in and out.

"Harder," she groaned, raking her nails down my back and digging her feet into my ass.

I gripped her hips and yanked her up as I surged down on each thrust. I was pissed that she wasn't coming on my trip with me, and I took my frustration out on her the only way I could think of – by fucking the shit out of her. I wasn't usually this rough with Alexa but her reactions were telling me that she liked it a lot. I'd have to keep that in mind in the future.

"One more. Give me one more, Alexa," I growled before I leveled myself up so I could brace an arm on the bed while I reached around with my other hand to pinch her clit. Her walls fluttered against me.

"So good," she groaned into my ear before nipping at the lobe and licking down my neck.

"The best," I agreed as I rolled my thumb over her nub. I circled my hips as I bottomed out on each thrust and my body clenched tightly as I felt my release start to roll through my body. And thank fuck that she started to tremble beneath me as I poured myself into her willing body.

"Drake," she gasped as I rode out her climax with small lunges, wanting to make this moment last as long as possible.

"That's it, baby. Give me what I need," I urged her on, knowing how much she loved to hear my raspy voice in her ear as she came. As her shudders ended, I rolled to my side and pulled her body to mine.

Several minutes passed before either of us spoke. "I'm going to miss you so much. You know that, right?" she asked quietly.

"Yes," I sighed. I knew our separation was going to be as difficult for her as it was for me, but it didn't help me feel any less frustrated. "Come with me then."

"You know I can't," she sighed. "My dad needs me here. He's got too much going on right now for me to skip out on him. If he didn't, you know I'd jump at the chance to be your number one cheerleader in person."

I was getting ready to leave for a month with my rugby team. My schedule was going to be packed solid between training during the week and matches on the weekends. I would have no time available to come back to town to see Alexa and it was killing me. We hadn't been apart for anything other than an odd night here and there other than that one damned weekend when she'd left me. Although months had passed since then, it still ate at me that my temper had almost led to me losing her forever.

Even though I knew we were solid now, I was worried about being apart for so long. It's not like I thought anything bad was going to happen, but I knew myself well enough to know that this next month was going to be tough. I'd gotten used to having time with Alexa whenever I wanted and I didn't want to lose that now, but I needed to be with my team and she needed to be here. So I had to suck it up and deal. *It was only a month. How bad could it be?*

I must have gotten lost in my head longer than I realized because when I refocused on Alexa she was looking at me with a worried expression on her face. "Of course I know that," I rushed to offer reassurance, softly kissing her cheek and rubbing my nose along hers.

"It's not even a full month, only twenty-seven days and we'll talk every chance we get," she reminded me.

"You're already counting down the days?" I teased her.

Alexa raised up on an elbow so she could reach my mouth. "Not the days. The minutes," she whispered against my lips before kissing me. And I knew everything was going to be okay. This girl was mine and nothing was going to change that.

Chapter 2

Alexa

DO YOU KNOW how many minutes are in twenty-seven days? Thirty eight thousand eight hundred and eighty. Counting each one down until I saw Drake sounded romantic when I was snuggled beside him in bed after two amazing orgasms, but the reality of it totally sucked. Especially when there was strange shit going on that was starting to freak me out.

The first couple weeks flew by without any problems. I helped my dad at the airport and had my own charters booked every single day. I missed Drake a lot, but I didn't have time to think about it much until we talked each night. We'd fill each other in on what we'd been up to and then enjoy some phone sex that always left me wanting more.

But this week was different. Strange things were happening and they left me feeling unsettled. The calls started on Monday morning. At first I thought someone just had the wrong number, but they kept coming. Every morning started with one at exactly the same time. And I felt like I was being watched at the store the other day but when I scanned around me I didn't see anyone looking my way. I just knew that there was a voice in my head telling me something wasn't right. And I felt like crap for not sharing my worries with Drake when we'd talked the last few days but I didn't want to freak him out.

Luckily I had a lunch date with Aubrey today so I could get her take on what was going on. Crap, if I didn't bust my ass I was going to be late getting there! And nothing pissed my best friend off more than being left to wait in a restaurant, which cracked me up because she wasn't always the most punctual of people. Inevitably, if she sat alone long enough, some guy was bound to ask to join her and she wasn't interested in guys lately. Which was very odd to think considering Aubrey's dating history, but the pregnancy scare last year had totally freaked her out. So now our roles had flipped since I had Drake and she was avoiding guys like the plague.

There she was waiting for me at a table, her foot tapping nervously. Aubrey looked so different dressed for work at the bank with black dress slacks, sling back heels and a silver blouse. With her long blond hair pulled back from her face in a low ponytail, her startling blue eyes looked even bigger. Her dad had her working as a teller this summer. He'd told her if she wanted to join the family business she needed to learn it form the ground up and pay her dues. She'd really surprised him by agreeing and doing a great job so far this summer. She wanted to prove to him that she was more than just her daddy's little girl.

"Hey, thanks for ordering my drink," I greeted Aubrey as I sat down and gestured to what I was guessing was a Diet Coke sitting in front of me.

"You're welcome! I know I can take a whole hour for lunch, but I don't want to be late getting back. I hope you don't mind that I ordered lunch already too," she answered.

"Not at all! I'm sure you knew what to get me. It's not like we haven't eaten here together a million times before. How's it going at the bank?" I asked.

"Okay so far. I know everyone there, which is good and bad. It's nice to see familiar faces every day, but it sucks to know that people see me a certain way when I'm trying to get them to take me seriously."

We both knew very well that Aubrey hadn't earned a businesslike reputation. She was absolutely the best friend a girl could ask for, but being the only girl with three older brothers had left her a little spoiled. Her parents were happy to give her anything she asked for, so she hadn't really needed to be serious about much of anything before now. She was known around town as a social butterfly not a worker bee.

"You'll wear them down. They might not know it yet, but you are

5

definitely determined when you want something," I reminded her.

"I am," she agreed. "And I want Daddy to know that he can trust me with the business. He'd always planned on handing the reins over to Jackson, but who knows when he'll be back from New York. It all depends on what happens with Kaylie's dancing."

Aubrey was right. Jackson had changed his whole world for Kaylie. There was no way he was coming back home until she was ready to join him. And I hoped for her sake that it wasn't any time soon.

"Give it time, Aubrey. You've got this," I told her, completely convinced that she could accomplish anything she put her mind to.

"Enough about me and my work troubles. What's going on with you? Why do you look so exhausted? I know it's gotta be tough with Drake gone, but I swear your eye bags have their own bags under them."

I heaved a deep sigh before describing the recent mysterious events. "Shit, Lexi! That sounds like the type of crap that Brad used to pull before he left town. This isn't good at all."

"You don't think I'm overreacting?" I asked, worried that my past bad experiences were making me prone to jumping to the wrong conclusion this time around.

"What does Drake have to say about all this?" Aubrey asked.

"Ummmmm, nothing yet. I haven't exactly told him yet," I admitted.

"Alexa!" she hissed at me. "What the hell are you thinking? You can't keep something like this from him. He's gonna go ape shit if something happens and you didn't share your concerns with him. Hell, he'd flip his lid even if nothing at all happens."

"I know. I need to tell him. I didn't at first because I thought maybe it was nothing, and I didn't want him to worry about me when he should be focusing on rugby. But if you agree that it sounds bad, then I promise to say something soon. After his games this weekend, okay?"

"No, I think you need to tell him now. I don't like this one bit and he won't either," she warned.

"This weekend is really important to the team and you know how much rugby means to him and his dad. I don't want to mess that up for Drake. His head wouldn't be in the game at all if he was thinking about what was happening here with me instead," I tried to explain.

"Nothing is more important to Drake than your safety, Lexi. You know how much you mean to him."

"Yes, I'm aware that he would come running in a heartbeat if he thought I needed him. That's why I need to be careful because I don't want him to mess up his future if this turns out to be nothing. Now, enough of this depressing talk. Let's hurry up and eat," I said gesturing at the waitress who was walking over with our order. "We've got to make sure you make it back to the bank on time."

Aubrey let me change the subject as we wolfed down our food and she told me about her parent's upcoming anniversary party. Before I knew it, the time had come for us to leave so she could head to work and I could go over to the airport to work on some paperwork for my dad before my flight.

As I walked to my Mini Cooper, I saw a white rose resting on the windshield and froze in my tracks. It completely freaked me out, but I didn't want Aubrey to see it yet. Not until I could figure out what the hell was going on. I swiveled my head to make sure she was almost to her car and I snagged the flower from the car and dropped it to the ground. I stomped on it in frustration, tears welling in my eyes. I wasn't going to go through this shit again. When everything went to hell with Brad, I was so relieved when he finally gave up and left town.

This just didn't make any sense to me. Was he back? And if so did he really think he had a chance in hell of getting me back? Drake had been gone for a few weeks now, so maybe he didn't know that I had a boyfriend now. There was only one thing I knew beyond a shadow of a doubt - Drake was going to go crazy when he found out what was going on.

Chapter 3

Drake

SOMETHING WAS WRONG with Alexa. I knew it deep in my bones. She tried to act like everything was okay, but she was acting weird during our calls whenever I asked how her day had gone. I wasn't sure what the fuck was going on, but it was starting to drive me crazy and mess with my head. It wasn't that I thought she was cheating on me or anything like that, but she was definitely hiding something from me. I just couldn't figure out what it could be and I was stuck here for another week before I could hunt her down and make her tell me.

She had gotten a lot better at sharing with me, but communication wasn't her strong suit. Sometimes it felt like I still had to pull the most important stuff out of her even though she knew she was safe with me. It drove me crazy, but we were working on it together. I just wish it wasn't taking so damn long for us to get better at this.

"Dude, what the fuck's wrong with you?" Lance, one of my line mates asked me. "You can't have another shit game like that and keep your place on the first line forever. You need to pull your head outta your ass and fast."

"I know man. It won't happen again," I promised.

"It's your chick, isn't it? She has you so wrapped. Just pick up some strange tonight at the bar and work out some of your frustration. She never has to know. What happens on the road stays on the road," he reminded me, raising his fist for a bump. Like I'd go for that shit with the crap he was talking. I just shook my head and walked away. I paused to glance at my phone when it rang and was surprised to see that it was Aubrey.

"Is she okay?" I asked as soon as I picked up the call.

The pause on the other line freaked me out and I started to walk faster to my car. "She's fine. Or at least I think she is, except she's going to kill me for calling you."

I beeped the locks and levered myself inside. "What's going on? It's got to be bad for you to call me instead of just talking Alexa into doing it herself."

"I had lunch with her on Friday," Aubrey started as she told me everything Lexi had shared with her a couple days earlier. "And I don't think she realized I saw, but I saw her pick something white up off her car and drop it on the ground. I didn't get a chance to go back until yesterday morning when I met my mom for lunch. And I found crushed white rose petals and a very thorny stem on the ground by where she had parked."

"Fuck," I swore.

"So I called Jackson to ask him for advice and he told me I better call you and make sure you knew," she continued.

"And what did Alexa have to say about why she hasn't called me herself?" I asked Aubrey, hoping for some insight into my girlfriend's thoughts since I was completely stumped as to why the hell she hadn't let me know what was going on already.

"Honestly, I think she was in denial at first. Worried that she was blowing the whole thing up in her head because of everything that happened with Brad before," she explained.

"And now?"

"She's scared to ruin your chances with the rugby team," Aubrey replied. "And I think she's a little worried that you might flip out and do something stupid to protect her. So you need to show her that she doesn't need to worry about shit like that with you. That you're smart enough to keep her covered without messing up your own stuff."

I didn't reply as I struggled with my desire to start the car and hit the road right then and there. But Aubrey was right, Alexa would let the guilt eat her alive if I just up and left without a word to coach and lost my place on the team.

"Did you hear what I said, Drake?" Aubrey asked.

"Yeah, I got you Aubrey. Don't worry. I'll figure out a way to get back without screwing everything up here. I've only got four more days of practices anyway, so I should be able to talk my way out with a family emergency or something."

"I went out on a limb here, calling you like this. Don't make me regret going behind Lexi's back to tell you what's going on," Aubrey warned. "I never would have done it if I wasn't so freaked out by what this could mean and what could go wrong. She needs you."

"Then she has me," I swore before hanging up and calling my dad for help.

"Hey Drake! How was the game?" he asked as he picked up the call.

"It was fine. We won, but I've got a problem, Dad," I answered before explaining what was going on with Alexa.

"That does sound like it could be a problem. Do you want to ask her if she wants to fly out here to stay with us?" he offered.

"No, Dad. I need to figure out who's at the bottom of this. As much as I'd like to just pull her out of her hometown and away from possible danger, it won't work in the long-run because we've got to go back to school in a few weeks anyway," I pointed out.

"That's a good point. I know a guy I can call for advice. He's done some work for me before. I think you've even met him a few times. I'm sure he'll know what to do. I'll give him a call to see what he thinks our next move should be. So don't go running off half-cocked until you hear back from me, okay?" he asked.

"I'm not making any promises, Dad. I'll head over to talk to Coach and get out of this week's practices so I can head back early. If I hit the road tonight, I can drive through the night and make it back into town tomorrow."

"I recognize that tone of voice, so I know there's no changing your mind. Just promise me you'll drive safely and have your coach call me if he gives you any trouble about leaving early," he offered. "I'll call you back as soon as I can to let you know what Nico has to say."

With a plan in place, I felt some of the weight lift from my shoulders. My dad had my back so I could have Alexa's - exactly how it should be.

Chapter 4

Alexa

I'D FINALLY GIVEN into my exhaustion and taken a Tylenol PM before going to bed, so the ringing of my phone confused me at first. I thought it was coming from my dream, but the sound was persistent. I reached a hand out to blindly search for my phone which was resting next to me on my bed for when Drake called me. I'd gone to bed pretty early, but I didn't want to miss his call.

"Hello," I murmured into the line when I managed to grab it. I blearily rubbed at my eyes when there was no reply, trying to peer at the screen to figure out if I'd missed catching him in time. Only the call was connected and it said *Unavailable* instead of Drake's name. Before I could say anything else the caller hung up and I realized that I'd somehow slept through ten missed calls. Back to back to back. All of them showing an unavailable phone number.

I was officially freaked out. My dad was gone for the next week on a trip for a company who used him for charters a lot, so I was alone in the house and suddenly I didn't feel very safe. What I wouldn't give for Drake to be here with me right now, but I knew those thoughts were purely selfish. He was exactly where he needed to be, but I definitely needed to tell him what was going on the next time we talked.

My phone rang again and I grabbed it and punched the green button without thinking first. "Who the hell is this?" I screamed into the phone.

"Alexa, it's me. What the hell's going on? Are you okay?" Drake asked on the other end of the line.

"Oh thank God," I sobbed into the phone hysterically. Between the tension of the last week, the medicine I'd taken to help me sleep and seeing those calls on my phone, I completely lost it.

"Shhh, baby. Everything's going to be okay. I promise," Drake soothed me. "Calm down. Tell me what happened."

Everything tumbled out from me in a rambling explanation. The calls, the flower, the weird feeling of being watched, my sudden fear at being home alone tonight. All of it.

"Alexa," he sighed. "We're going to have a serious conversation later about why you waited to talk to me about this. But for now I want you to go downstairs and make sure the doors and windows are locked and the alarm is set."

"Okay," I whispered, ashamed at the disappointment I heard in his tone.

"Do it now while I'm on the phone with you, baby. I want to make sure you're safe tonight."

I wandered downstairs and made sure everything was locked up. I hardly ever used the alarm system my dad had put in because he wanted me to be secure when he traveled out of town overnight, but I was relieved that he'd had it put in now.

"All done," I said as I climbed back into bed and pulled the blankets over my head to shut the rest of the world out.

"Good," Drake replied before there was silence on the line.

It was a deafening silence that made me worry Drake was pissed and wouldn't forgive me for not telling him about everything right away. "Are you mad at me?" I asked.

Drake didn't answer right away. I felt the tension mounting between us. "I'm not happy with you right now," he admitted. "But we can talk about that later. You need to get some sleep."

"I'm sorry," I whispered , my words slurring slightly as my sleepiness overcame me again.

"I know you are, baby. Everything will be okay. Sleep now," he murmured into the line as I felt myself drift off.

THE SUNLIGHT WAS streaming through my bedroom window when I woke up the next morning. I still felt fuzzy since I always reacted weird to Tylenol PM. I couldn't even take a full pill, I had cut one in half last night. As I rolled over onto my phone, I realized that the last thing I remembered was talking to Drake about him being angry with me for keeping stuff from him. And rightly so. I didn't know what I had been thinking. I should have mentioned it after the first phone call. Or at least when it happened the second morning. Definitely on the third. By then it was a pattern that I couldn't ignore.

Burying my head in the sand wasn't going to help anything. It seemed like whatever was going on was just getting worse. The call last night threw me since it wasn't in the morning like the others. And the flower on my car freaked me out. I needed to figure out what the hell was going on here, but I didn't have any idea where to even begin other than maybe to call the Sheriff's office. I definitely need to talk to my dad and Drake about it too.

I made some coffee to help wake myself up and wandered out onto the front porch as soon as I was able to pour myself a cup. With my first step outside I realized something was wrong. A bunch of white roses rested on the doorstep. That meant that the person who had been calling had been to my house this morning first thing before I woke up and left them for me.

I stared at the flowers for a moment before picking them up and tearing them apart in search of a card. There had to be something here that would tell me who had sent them. I needed a sign, a clue, anything to tell me who was behind this all.

As I was flinging flowers out of the package, the sound of a car turning into the drive startled me. I glanced up and saw Drake's Viper pulling up to the house. The staggering relief that I felt at seeing him, even knowing that it meant he left early and drove through the night to me, almost brought me to my knees. I ran towards him and flung myself into his arms as soon as he stepped out of the car. Even with everything hanging over my head, I'd never felt safer than I did with his arms wrapped tightly around me.

Chapter 5

Drake

I HAD PUSHED MY car to the limit to make my way back to Alexa as fast as I possibly could, stopping only for a few quick pit stops. My focus was completely on the drive ahead of me and trying to keep my temper in check. I hadn't liked the advice my dad had given me when he called back. I liked it even less right now. How in the hell was I supposed to keep a level head when some ass was playing games with my girl?

When she broke down during our call last night, I knew beyond a shadow of a doubt that I'd made the right decision in leaving early to be here for her. Having her in my arms right now only reinforced that feeling. I carried her upstairs to her room and dropped her onto her feet before I noticed the rose petals in her hair.

"What the hell?" I growled, gesturing at her head. I watched as she reached up and pulled a petal away.

"I found them outside this morning," she explained. "But I have no idea who sent them. I couldn't find a card or anything."

I was pissed the hell off that someone was tormenting my girl and frustrated beyond measure that things had gone this far without her telling me anything. "Dammit, Alexa. You can't keep shit like this from me."

"I'm sorry, Drake. I was going to tell you what was going on. I swear I was. At first it was just little things and I didn't want to worry you. I didn't realize that it was so serious and by then you were already here."

"Goddamit, Alexa!" I roared. "When are you going to get it? If you've got a problem, then I've got one too! You are mine! Mine to fuck. Mine to love. And mine to protect!"

"Yes, I'm yours," she tried to soothe the beast that was roaring inside me, but mere words weren't going to cut it.

"Strip," I bit out as I ripped my shirt over my head. She looked at me with a stunned expression on her beautiful face. "Now!" I ordered because she wasn't moving fast enough. The need to dominate her was riding me hard.

As soon as she was down to her panties I tossed her onto the bed and rolled her onto her stomach. I pulled her panties to the side and lifted her ass in the air so I could feast on her from behind. At the first flick of my tongue I heard her sigh deeply. Stiffening my tongue, I fucked in and out of her body while I roughly held her in place with a tight grip on the crease at the top of her legs.

I hadn't shaved in days, and my scruff was scraping against the sensitive skin between her thighs. The red marks on her skin, a stamp of my possession, soothed me a little. But it wasn't enough. I dipped two fingers inside to make sure she was ready. Thank fuck she always wanted me because I found her dripping wet so I drove in with one powerful thrust.

"Do you trust me baby?" I groaned.

"Yes," she gasped out her answer as I drilled her with measured strokes.

"When you don't talk to me about shit, it makes me feel like you don't trust me," I growled.

"No, Drake. That wasn't it at all," she whimpered, whipping her head back and forth.

"I don't know if I believe you baby. Do you really trust me that much?" I goaded her.

"Yes! You have to know I do. With everything. Anything."

A dark chuckle escaped from my lips as an idea formed in my head. A way to prove that she had complete faith in me. "Give me your hands, Alexa."

"What?" she asked, a dazed look on her face as I held still behind her with my cock buried deep inside.

I pushed her shoulders down on the bed and drew her hands behind her back. I gripped them tightly in one fist and lifted one of her knees so I could fuck her slow and deep. "I know it's gonna hurt a little baby. I've never been this far before, but I need you to trust me to make it good for you. Can you do that for me, Alexa?"

"Yes," she hissed out.

"Fuck, just like that," I groaned as I bottomed out inside her bumping against her cervix. My balls slapped against her pussy with each thrust earning me a gasp every time. Her hair had slid over her face so I couldn't see her eyes anymore so I widened my knees to get more leverage and reached down to pull her hair away. Her walls clenched against me as I tugged it out of the way.

"More," she moaned so I grasped her hair in my fist and yanked it back as I pounded inside even harder.

"My baby likes being a little bad?" I grunted.

"Oh God," she screamed as she flew over the edge and clenched tight around me.

"Lift your ass higher for me," I growled as I tugged her hair more tightly in my fist and pulled her fists up a little to make room for her to follow my command.

With her body spread out below me, completely at my mercy, I knew she got my point. I grabbed Lexi's hips as I hammered inside, over and over again. Each punishing thrust a reminder of who she belonged to. Me.

Chapter 6

Alexa

A S I STARED out the kitchen window, sipping my coffee, I pondered how the last couple days went by without too much trouble. Having Drake around made me feel less vulnerable. Some women might judge me for it since I should be able to take care of myself, but part of what drew me to Drake in the first place was how safe he made me feel. But I never expected to be in the kind of situation where he would find the need to take it to the extreme.

I wasn't allowed to go anywhere by myself. And since my dad wasn't back in town yet, that meant that Drake took me everywhere. Hell, I was surprised I was able to convince him to let me take a plane up without him. Thank God for that because that would be super awkward with a Mile High Club Flight. Hello paying customers who want to get some alone time in the back of my plane. Don't mind my boyfriend sitting up here with me. I promise he's not a Peeping Tom, he doesn't plan to video tape you, and no he's not available to join you either. I was pretty sure that wouldn't have gone over very well at all.

He also added a ton of bells and whistles to the security system my dad had installed a few years ago. We now had motion detectors inside the house that would trip the alarm if someone made it into the house. How they'd manage that with the motion sensor lights, glassbreak detectors and panic buttons he'd also had put in I had no idea. Add in hidden security cameras so that Drake would be able to catch someone if they approached the house when they weren't supposed to be there and I felt like I was starring in my favorite movie. Although, I don't think even Mark Wahlberg would be able to come up with a plan to get in here if I was hiding gold bars in the basement.

This waiting game was beginning to drive us both crazy. Nothing had happened since Drake came into town. I wasn't sure if I felt better because maybe it was over or worse because it could mean that they were watching me closely enough to know that Drake was with me now. I almost wanted something to happen so we could bring this mess to an end and move on, hopefully with a little more freedom for me.

"Hey, baby," Drake whispered in my ear as he wrapped his arms around me.

I'd left him sound asleep in my bed. In the room I'd grown up in. Where my stuffed animals and dolls rested next to trophies and awards. A room that will never seem innocent to me after the things Drake has done to my body in that bed. Just the thought of what we'd done together had a blush spreading across my body.

"Mmmmm, what's put that look on your face?" Drake teased before nipping at my ear.

I turned in his arms to kiss him good morning. "Well," I began before I was interrupted by the sound of my cell phone ringing. "That's weird. It's Aubrey, but she should be at work already."

"Then you'd better grab it in case it's something important," Drake said before giving me a quick, hard kiss on the lips and stepping away to root around in the fridge for stuff to make breakfast.

"Hey, what's up?" I answered the line.

"Lexi, you are not going to believe who I just saw at the bank. Or I think I saw because as soon as he saw me he turned around and left right away," she babbled on without getting to the point.

"Aubrey!" I interrupted her. "Who the hell was it?"

"Shit, sorry. I could swear it was Brad."

"Brad?" I gasped, drawing Drake's attention back to me. "Yeah, I can't be sure because he took off so quickly. But I really think it was him," she said. "Do you think he's behind the strange crap that's been going on?"

18

"I don't know," I whispered, staring at Drake with a look of horror upon my face.

He slammed the refrigerator door closed and stomped over to me, grabbing the phone from my hand. "What the hell Aubrey?" he growled into the line. I watched as a variety of expressions crossed his face – understanding, anger, and even a flash of satisfaction. "Don't worry. I've got her covered. Thanks for letting us know, though."

He paused to listen to what Aubrey had to say for a moment. "Yeah, I get that you aren't sure if it was him or not, but at least you've given me somewhere to look. I'll make some calls, find out if he's in town or not. It's good to finally have an idea of who the fuck might be behind this shit."

I pressed myself against Drake's body, wanting to get as close as possible. "You don't have to do that. Stay where you are. Act like you didn't see anything wrong and let me do my thing. Trust me. There's no way in hell I will let anything happen to my Lexi."

Drake punctuated this statement with a kiss to the top of my head as he disconnected the call. I was shaking in his arms, relieved to finally have an idea of what had been going on but scared by what this could mean. I thought things with Brad had ended back when the Silvers got him to leave town. Why would he be back and causing problems for me now? It had been ages since I had last seen him.

"This is a good thing, baby. Knowing where to look will help us end this sooner. You know that, right?" Drake asked.

My head was buried in his chest. "I know," I mumbled.

"Hey, look at me Alexa," Drake commanded as he tilted my head up and looked me in the eyes. "What's going on in that pretty head of yours?"

I felt tears well up in my eyes and spill down my cheeks. "I feel like such an idiot. It never even crossed my mind that it could be Brad, even though he pulled crap like this before he left town. That's why Jackson felt the need to push him into leaving. So he wouldn't bother me anymore."

"No, he doesn't get to make you feel bad. Not about this. There was no reason for you to think it was him this time. You had no idea he was even in town for fucks sake," he growled as he wiped the tears from my face. "He doesn't deserve your tears. Or anything of yours anymore. You're mine and he's going to learn that lesson very soon. Now go wash up while I make a couple calls, okay?"

I searched his eyes for any sign that his anger was directed at me since

I kinda felt like this whole situation was my fault. If I hadn't been an idiot and dated the loser in the first place, we wouldn't be going through this now. I was relieved when I realized Drake was pissed for me and not at me. He wasn't looking at me any differently than he normally did. "Love you," I whispered to him before turning to walk upstairs and wash my face.

I wasn't gone very long, and Drake was on the phone when I came back downstairs.

"Fuck, Nico. I finally have a lead on who's been messing around with Alexa's head. Turns out her ex-boyfriend is back in town and Jackson thinks this is exactly the type of shit he would pull. But things are escalating and I need to move fast before he has a chance to get at her," he grumbled.

Drake paused to listen to whatever was being said on the other end of the call. "Godammit! I know you get where I'm coming from here, man. What I want to do is hunt this bastard down and beat the shit out of him. Rips his balls off and shove them down his throat. It shouldn't be too hard to find him. Give me five minutes with him and this could all be over in a heartbeat."

Whatever he heard before the call ended didn't seem to make Drake any happier since he threw his phone against the wall instead of just hanging up. "Fuck!"

I ran over and picked up the pieces to see if it was salvageable, but there was no way his phone was ever going to work again. "Looks like we need to make a stop at the Verizon store first thing to get you a new phone," I pointed out unnecessarily, looking for a way to end the silence.

"Shit, babe. Sorry about that."

"No big deal," I reassured him. "Throw as many phones as you want. It's not like I haven't killed my fair share of phones, too."

My reminder of the my bad luck with cell phones made him chuckle and lightened the mood a little. "Yeah, you better watch out or I'll take your place as the phone assassin. Only your preferred method is death by drowning."

And he was right. If there was a body of water near my phone and me, I had to be super careful. I could personally vouch that the bag of rice method of drying out a phone only worked so many times before it would just give up the ghost. "You better watch out or the next one I drop into a glass of ice water will be yours," I warned him.

He smirked in response, reminded of the last phone I'd killed. "I'll make sure not to let you use mine the next time you're drunk and I make you drink some. Or at least I'll grab the phone out of the water instead of watching you stare at it like you have no idea what you're seeing. Damn that shit was funny."

I smacked his arm in response. "Yeah, until the next morning when I realized my phone was dead and I thought I would have to make it until Monday without one."

"Only you didn't because I took care of it," he reminded me. "Just like I'll take care of my phone this time. And I'll take care of this mess with Brad. I'll always take care of you Alexa. You know that, right?"

My heart practically burst at the seams when I saw how serious Drake was. If I didn't already know that he would do just about anything for me, his intense stare would certainly get the point across now. I nodded my head and sighed deeply at the realization that I didn't have to be scared of anything with Drake at my side.

Chapter 7

Drake

B Y THE END of the day, I'd been able to confirm that Alexa's ex was back in town. His parents had moved within the last year, so nobody knew why he was here. I didn't like that we'd lost leverage against him with them moving. He probably thought he didn't have anything to lose when he decided to come back because the Silvers couldn't threaten their home since it was sold. Little did he know that my family's reach spread much further. If I wanted to destroy him financially, there wasn't anything that would stand in my way.

He was booked into a local hotel, but nobody had seen him all day. I figured he was spooked when he recognized Aubrey at the bank. His choice to get out of there right away instead of stopping to talk to her made it pretty damn clear that he was the one behind everything, too. Now I just needed to find him. Who knew how difficult that would be in a town this small?

Alexa wasn't super happy with me because I'd insisted that she stay close to home today. I couldn't shake the feeling that things were about to come to a head, and with all the improvements to the security system here I felt like this was the safest place for her. I knew she felt like I was going overboard, but if I could have gotten away with building a ten-foot gated fence around the house, I would have done that too. Then she'd have a reason to feel like I went too far.

I glanced across the bed at her, relieved that she seemed to be sleeping so soundly. She'd tossed and turned every night so far, but tonight she fell fast asleep in my arms like she didn't have a worry in the world. Maybe she was finally getting it and knew that she would always be safe with me. No matter what.

Unfortunately, it didn't seem like I was going to get much rest tonight. I was too jazzed up knowing that I'd set things in motion to bring this trouble with Brad to an end. I figured that the call my dad had made to his parents would either push him over the edge and get him to do something stupid or would get him to back off completely. Either option was fine by me as long as this ended with Alexa safe and sound beside me.

I had finally drifted off to sleep when the flood light I'd had installed at the front porch turned on, quickly followed by a pounding at the door.

"Alexa!" I heard someone bellow. "Open up!"

Lexi rolled over in her sleep and mumbled under her breath at the noise. I quickly launched myself out of bed and headed downstairs. It sounded like I'd finally get the chance to meet her bastard of an ex-boy-friend after all. I wasn't fast enough and he pounded on the door again like a crazy man. I chuckled darkly as I realized this was going to work perfectly since the cameras would have turned on the second he stepped onto the porch. I disabled the alarm and opened the door.

"Dude, this is not cool. You're going to wake Alexa up, and you've already stolen enough sleep from her this week. Quiet down," I growled softly at him with a glance up the stairs.

"Fuck you," he slurred. "I don't know who the hell you think you are, but you better get Alexa's ass down here now. Fucking bitch thinks she can just mess up my whole life."

"No way man. It's the middle of the night and she's sleeping. Even if she wasn't, there's no way I'm gonna let some guy call my woman a bitch and then let him into her house to talk to her," I said, standing with my arms crossed in front of me. I made sure to block his way into the house. I wasn't going to make this easy for him. Not even a little bit.

"Get outta my fucking way," he said as he shoved at me, barely moving me an inch.

"Not gonna happen. Why don't you walk away, cool down and come back tomorrow when she's awake and you're prepared to act like a reasonable adult?" I offered. "You smell like a brewery. Don't do something you'll regret later because you've had too much to drink to know better."

"Fuck yeah, I've been drinking. She's out to ruin me. Just because I got some on the side back when we were dating, she can't let it go. I tried making amends. Left her roses, her favorite. Did that soften her up? No – she had to call in the big dogs to go after my parents instead of just forgiving me," he rambled on drunkenly.

"Drake? What's going on?" I heard Alexa murmur sleepily from behind me. I swiveled my head to find her standing at the bottom of the stairs. At least she'd had the good sense to throw one of my button-down shirts on over her nightie.

"Nothing for you to worry about, baby. Go back upstairs," I turned towards her as I answered, giving Brad the chance to push past me into the house. And now his ass was mine.

"What the fuck, Alexa? You're too good to talk to me now? I left town like you wanted me to before. Why do you have to be such a bitch about me coming back now?" Brad lit into her.

"Me? A bitch?" she gasped. "I didn't even know you were back until today."

"Well you certainly didn't welcome me back with open arms. And you moved damn fast to have your friends threaten me again," he accused. "You need to call your fucking dogs off. I'm tired of the Silvers sticking their noses into my business just because Jackson wants in your panties," he ranted.

"Don't be ridiculous. I did no such thing!" she argued as she stepped further closer to us. I shook my head and took a couple steps to place myself between her and Brad as she paused at the bottom of the stairs.

"Then who the hell called my parents to warn them about me backing off and leaving you alone?" he yelled.

I heard Alexa groan as I turned to him to answer for her. I guess now she knew some of what I'd been up to today. "That would be me."

"What, you've got a new douche-bag in your life who can't stand the fact that you gave it up to me?" he taunted.

"The douche is going to be her husband, so why don't you stop talking to my woman and hash this out with me, man?" I demanded.

"Whatever dude. She was my woman first and if I want to talk to her then I will," he argued as he tried to get past me again to reach Alexa.

"I don't give a fuck who the hell you think you are or what you once were to her. Make no mistake. She's mine now and you're not talking to her like this," I said as I pushed him back.

He stumbled a little and came up swinging. It was the perfect excuse for me to do exactly what I'd wanted from the second he knocked on the door. No, scratch that. From the minute I'd heard about the way he'd hurt my girl back when they were dating. Now he'd just given me more reason to beat his ass into the ground with his actions over the last week. So I laid him out with an uppercut to his chin. One punch and he went down. Fucking sissy.

"I warned you to stay away from her, but you just wouldn't listen. Would you?" I asked as I leaned over and gripped his shirt in my hands.

"Who are you to tell me what to do?"

"You really are dumb," I answered, punching him in the face again. "Didn't you hear me earlier. I'm the man who makes sure nothing bad touches her anymore. The one who's going to marry her and take care of her for the rest of her life. Clearly you aren't getting that so maybe I can knock some sense into you, dipshit."

He struggled, kicking out and swiping my legs out from underneath me. I made sure I landed on top of him, driving a knee into his side as I went down.

"Umph," he groaned. "Get off me!"

"Stay. The. Fuck. Away. From. My. Wife." Each word was punctuated with a punch in his ribs.

Brad was gasping for air underneath me, his arms wrapped around his torso for protection. "I was just trying to make amends, man."

I leaned down to glare into his eyes. "Then you're more of a dumbass than I thought you were. If you wanted to tell make up the shit you'd pulled in the past, you should of done it face to face without scaring her half to death with hang-up phone calls and mystery flowers."

Brad glanced over at her, and I forced his head my way so he was staring at me instead. "I didn't mean to scare her. I just kept losing my nerve when I heard her voice. And I figured she'd know who the flowers were from. She never dated anyone else after me. Who else would have given her flowers?"

"Then you missed something big, dude. She is dating someone else. And I don't care why you were here or what you were trying to do. Alexa isn't your concern anymore. She's mine. If you know what's good for you and your family, you will stay far, far away from her. You got that?"

I stepped away from him, confident that he finally got what I was saying. I was breathing heavily, worried that I'd just scared the shit out of Alexa by beating the crap out of him in front of her until she came up behind me rested her head on my back. Her arms sneaked around my waist. "My hero," she whispered, making me feel about ten feet tall. I should have known my girl wouldn't scare easily.

Chapter 8

Alexa

WHAT THE HELL *just happened?* I couldn't believe that every-thing was over. Brad had been led away in handcuffs. Drake had to answer some questions since he'd beaten the crap out of him, but since Brad had come onto my property without my permission and refused to leave, I was pretty sure we didn't have much to worry about.

Everyone had left and it was just the two of us. I felt like there was a giant elephant in the room because there was no way I could un-hear what Drake had just yelled at Brad while they were fighting. And I wasn't even sure if he realized he'd called me his wife. Or maybe he did since he had still been pretty calm when he'd said he was going to be my husband.

"So," I said hesitantly. "Your wife, huh?"

"Fuck," he growled and stomped out the front door to his car, totally freaking me out. He reached into the glove box and grabbed something from inside. He stormed back up the stairs, slamming the door behind him. "He might have fucked up my plan, but we aren't doing this down here. Not like this. Upstairs," he ordered.

I shook my head in confusion and before I knew it, Drake had picked me up in a fireman's hold and was marching up the stairs.

"Drake," I yelped.

"Calm down, baby. I've got you," he answered with a pat on my ass. As soon as we made it to my room, he tossed me on the bed. I leaned up on an elbow to find him dropping down onto his knees at the edge of the bed and pulling a small blue jewelry box out of his pocket.

"Ohimigod," I breathed out.

Drake glanced down at the floor before looking up and locking his eyes with mine. I knew he loved me. He had no problem showing me how much I meant to him each and every day in so many different ways. But his feelings had never more shown more clearly than right here, right now as his love blazed from his dark eyes.

"This isn't how I planned this at all," he started. "I wanted this moment to be romantic. Something you could tell our children and grandchildren about as we grow old together. But I don't think I can wait to ask, so I guess they're going to end up with a whole different story when we share how I popped the question."

I giggled in response as he pulled a gorgeous ring out of the box and pushed it onto my finger. "I don't recall hearing any questions being popped," I teased.

He shook his head at me before responding. "Alexa, will you be my wife? Let me love you and protect you for the rest of my days? Wear my ring so that nobody will ever doubt that you're mine?"

"Are you sure?" I asked, worried that this was just a heat of the moment decision.

"Lexi, baby. I bought this ring months and months ago," he said as he rubbed his finger across the ring that was nestled on my finger. "If I'd thought you were ready, you would have been wearing it at Christmas."

"You've had it that long?" I asked, shocked to hear that he'd been thinking about marriage when I'd had no idea.

"Longer," he answered. I smiled at him, with tears running down my cheeks and nodded. "I don't recall hearing an answer," he teased.

"Yes!" I shrieked as I threw myself off the bed and into his arms. "A million times yes."

HOLD YOUR HORSES

(Blythe College 2.5)

by Rochelle Paige

PROLOGUE

Charlotte

I WATCHED KAYLIE AS she scoured the internet in search of an apartment for her and Jackson's move to New York and couldn't help but feel a little irritated at her excitement. I knew it made me a bitch, but I just couldn't stop myself from feeling this way. Graduation was just around the corner, and she had a plan for what she was going to do, where she was going to do it, and who she was going to be with while she was doing it. At the start of the semester, she'd had no clue, but everything had just fallen into place for her since she met Jackson. He'd worked hard to make sure that it had done so.

Don't get me wrong. I was beyond thrilled that Kaylie had found Jackson. That he had managed to break down her walls and get her to see that life was worth living again. I wanted the best that life had to offer for my best friend. I really did. I just wanted it for myself too.

I couldn't wrap my head around the decision I needed to make. After four long years, Shane couldn't wait to get me back home so that we could finally be together without the distance that had separated us for so long. And I wanted to be with him so much. Both of us had put a lot of effort into making sure our relationship survived while I was away at school. And now that there was a light at the end of the tunnel, I just wasn't sure that I wanted to go back home and live my life in our small Tennessee hometown.

Moving there the summer before my senior year of high school had been difficult for me, but my parents had to do what was right for our whole family. My parents had inherited the bar from a great-uncle we hardly even knew, my Nanny's brother. And boy, doesn't that make us really Southern, calling my grandma Nanny because her name is Annie. As if having six siblings didn't make us hillbilly enough when I was growing up in Knoxville, Tennessee. When my parents found out he had left them a huge, rambling house along with the bar, it was a no-brainer for them. They moved us all a little farther south to a much smaller town where everyone knew each other because their families had lived there forever. And I got to spend my final year of high school feeling like an outsider before I headed out of town for college.

The one bright spot while I was there was Shane. I met him my first week of school and was instantly smitten. Not that I let him know how into him I was right away. He was the guy that every girl wanted, so I had to play hard to get just a teensy bit. He sure did make the chase worth my while once he caught me. Unfortunately, that just gave the other girls at school a reason not to like me other than my not growing up there with all of them.

They sure didn't warm up to me when Shane and I continued to date while I was away at school either. I was the outsider who'd swooped in and stolen their most eligible bachelor away and then had the gall to go to college out of state without letting him go. Which led me to my current problem—did I really want to spend the rest of my life around people who had made it clear that they thought I didn't belong in their town and that I certainly didn't deserve to be with Shane?

CHAPTER
One

Shane

AFTER FOUR LONG years, the time had finally come for Charlotte to graduate from college. There had been times over the years that I'd wanted to jump into my pickup truck and drag her ass back home where it belonged—with me. But how could I have done that when I'd known damn well that she wouldn't be happy without earning that piece of paper that meant so much to her parents? She was the oldest and they wanted her to set an example for her younger brothers and sisters. And if it had just been that, I might not have resisted the urge to go get her, but I'd also known that she'd needed the time away from this town to spread her wings so she would be ready to come back to me and settle down.

People around these parts didn't always take to newcomers very quickly, so things had been tough for Char when she moved here as a senior in high school. I was pretty sure I hadn't made things any easier for her by setting my sights on her right away either. The girls didn't like that I had gone after her like a dog in heat, but shit if I could have helped myself. She had been so different from all the other girls, not giving a damn that I was interested until I made her pay attention. She'd made me work for it, and I'd enjoyed the chase a helluva lot.

Maybe if any of the other girls around these parts hadn't been so damn easy, I would have wanted one of them instead, but I didn't think so. There was just something about my sassy redheaded girl that made every part of me stand up and take notice. Before I knew it, she had me wrapped around her finger and acting like a pussy-whipped fool. Hell, she had me doing all sorts of things that were out of character—like agreeing to a long-distance relationship so I wouldn't lose her. I'd never been good at waiting. But for Char, I'd wait just about forever.

Hell, she had even gotten me into a suit for today. I was stuck sitting here in the audience with the sun beaming down on me in a damn monkey suit, waiting for her to walk across the stage to get her diploma. At least I hadn't budged on wearing my boots. I'd even agreed to give her youngest sister a ride in the truck all the way up here when she had turned those bright green eyes at me with a huge pout on her face that made me think of Char. I just hadn't been able say no, even though it'd meant I had to drive slower and didn't get here in time to see my girl before she had to be here with the rest of her class. So I sent her a quick text before we hit the road to wish her luck today because I wasn't going to get to see her until it was all over. She promised to make it up to me since she knew how happy I had made her sister. And boy, did Char know how to make things up to me. I could almost picture her on her knees in front of me, her hair fisted in my hands as she wrapped her lips around my cock.

I tried to adjust myself as subtly as I could now that I'd managed to give myself the hard-on from hell. Fuck, I couldn't think about that right now, sitting here surrounded by her family. But it had been almost two months since we had been together. Those damn Skype calls just didn't cut it when we had to go without for so long. Sure, they were fun and sexy and they helped us get over the dry spell, but it just wasn't the same as sinking inside of her. And there I went again, except now I was picturing my dick in her pussy instead of her mouth. I had no fucking idea how the hell I was supposed to make it through the day without getting at least a little taste of her, but I was pretty sure it wasn't going to happen. Not until I could get her alone back home. This was going to be one of the longest days of my life. And that was saying a lot considering how slowly the last four years had crept by.

The sound of Char's name being announced ripped me out of my fog. I leaned forward a bit, determined not to miss a moment of her walk across stage. She looked fantastic, even in that ridiculous robe and cap. Her red hair flowed down her back, a huge smile was spread across her face, and her legs looked incredible in the black fuck-me heels she was wearing. I glanced over at her mom and saw tears streaming down her cheeks. Her dad stood next to her, hooting and hollering wildly for his baby girl. I jumped to my feet to join in and realized we were probably embarrassing the shit out of her, but it didn't matter. I wasn't the only one excited to have her come back home.

I WAITED WITH everyone once graduation was over, and Char launched herself into my arms first thing.

"Hey, sugar," I whispered into her ear, holding her tight against my body. I didn't want to let her go, but I knew she needed to say hi to everyone else too. I slowly released her to set her back on the ground.

She shook her head when she realized her mom was still crying and headed over to her dad next.

"Aren't you happy to see your daddy?" he teased as she gave him a big hug.

He winked at me over her shoulder, already used to how his daughter and I were around each other. At least enough that I didn't have to worry about him coming after me with his shotgun anymore. Somewhere around the two-year mark, he'd realized I was sticking around and started to cut me some slack.

"Of course I am, Daddy," she sighed.

"I know where I rank on your list, sweetie," he joked.

"Right where you belong," her mom chimed in, bumping him out of the way to wrap her arms around Char. "I'm so proud of you, honey. I can hardly believe it. My little girl graduated from college today."

"Oh, Mama. Stop! No more tears today," Char chided before her brothers and sisters offered with their congratulations too.

"Now you know your mama is gonna cry as much as she wants. There's no stopping her once the water works start," her dad reminded.

"Very true," Char agreed. "But today should be about celebrating the fact that I survived college. No tears allowed."

"They're happy tears, sweetie," her mom murmured as she pulled her back in for another hug. "Very happy ones. I finally get my baby girl to come back home. I know I agreed it was best for you to go away to school, but I've just missed you so much. I can hardly wait to have my baby girl living under my roof again."

An odd look crossed Char's face at her mom's words—a flash of concern that made me wonder if she knew about the ring in my pocket. If I had my way, her mom wouldn't have her home for very long. She'd get to see her a lot more than when Char was up here for school, but I wanted us to start our life together so that I could wake up to her in my bed each and every morning.

I glanced over at her dad and caught him watching me with a knowing look on his face. I didn't think he was going to be surprised by my plans. His next words gave me hope that he'd be in my corner.

"Now why don't we help our girl get her stuff packed up into the back of Shane's truck before we head out to celebrate at supper?" he asked.

"Sounds like a plan to me," I answered just before I heard someone shrieking Char's name and turned to find her roommate Kaylie coming towards us, dragging her boyfriend Jackson behind her.

"Hi, everyone!" she said as she stopped to give each person in Char's family a quick hug before wrapping her arms around Char and bursting into tears. "I can't believe we aren't going to be roomies anymore!"

"Hey!" Jackson protested. "What am I? Chopped liver?"

"Yeah, Kaylie. You're trading me in for the new and improved model. He comes with all sorts of upgrades that I don't," Char teased her.

"Damn straight I do," Jackson muttered under his breath, quiet enough so the kids didn't hear him, but I couldn't help myself from busting up laughing.

"I sure as hell hope so, man," I joked with him. I'd only met Jackson once over the last few months, but he was easy to get along with since he treated Kaylie so well, which made Char happy.

"I didn't mean it that way," Char pointed out as she nudged me in the ribs, blushing once she'd caught on to the direction our thoughts had gone.

"Okay, boys. Enough teasing Charlotte. We've got lots of things to get done today," her mom said, urging us to focus. "Kaylie, do you need help packing anything up, too?"

"Nope. Jackson has us covered, but we aren't going anywhere until tomorrow so we can help y'all for a little bit if you'd like," she offered.

"No helping for you, sweetie. We can't risk you getting hurt before you head to the Big Apple. I can hardly believe we'll be able to say we knew you when once your name is up there in lights," Char's mom said.

"Yeah, no helping for you," Jackson agreed. "You sit there looking pretty and I'll help Shane load up the truck. It will probably save us loads of time later too so you won't have to repair any damage you manage to do before we meet back up with my parents again. Are you sure you can't all stay for the open house at their place?"

"I really wish we could, but I've got to be up to work the horses in the morning," I declined.

"I wish we could, but we've got to make sure the kids are all back and ready to go for their last week of school, too," Char's mom added. "C'mon. You two can chat while we put the men to work. And you can always talk on Skype whenever you want, just like you did with Shane, so you can stay in touch with each other."

As we headed back to the dorm, the girls broke into giggles because of the mention of Skype since their calls would be quite a bit different from mine with Charlotte. No doubt about that, because I don't share my girl with anyone else.

C HAPTER Two

Charlotte

THE DRIVE BACK home was bittersweet. We'd packed everything up so quickly. Four long years' worth of stuff had been put into boxes to bring back home so very easily. Almost like those years away had never even happened. I'd said my final goodbyes to Kaylie, wrecking our makeup in the process because neither of us could stop crying at the thought of being halfway across the country from each other.

Dinner out with my family had been crazy as usual. Not that I should have expected anything less. It was impossible for it to be any other way when we were all together, everyone trying to talk at once. It had been really nice to be with my family again and to have Shane at my side, but I'd still felt sad as we'd pulled out of the restaurant parking lot to head back home. A chapter in my life was ending and I wasn't sure in which new direction I wanted to go yet.

The silence between us as I rode back with Shane was awkward—at least to me. He'd turned the radio on low, one soulful Southern song playing after another. My sister Molly had insisted on coming along with us, and she acted as the perfect buffer for me. I wasn't ready to explain what was going on in my head to Shane yet. I hadn't been able to figure it out myself yet and wasn't about to scare him if I didn't need to. I hoped like hell that once we got back home my nerves would go away. That it would feel like home to me in a way it never had before. The way that Shane felt like home to me.

"CHAR, WE'RE HERE."

Shane's whisper woke me up. I didn't remember when, but I must have fallen asleep at some point on the drive home. Molly was sprawled halfway in my lap, as much as her seatbelt would let her, while I was resting against Shane's shoulder.

"We're here already?" I asked as I realized we had pulled into the driveway of my parents' house. "Shit, I'm sorry you got stuck driving while we slept."

Shane leaned over and kissed my forehead before answering. "Like I didn't know that would happen anyway. You always fall asleep in the car unless we're just driving in town."

I loved that he knew that about me. That he pretty much knew everything there was to know about me and still loved me so much—little quirks and all. While I stretched, he hopped out of the truck and came around to the passenger's side to lift Molly out and carry her into the house. My parents' car was parked in front of us, and they must have beaten us home because it was already empty and the lights were on in the house.

By the time I managed to fully wake up, Shane was already back. I started to slide towards the passenger's side door, but he climbed back in that way and pushed me across the bench towards the driver's side. I glanced at the house nervously and saw the front porch light turn on before he grasped my face in his palms.

"Charlotte," he sighed as his lips crashed down on mine and every single thought flew out of my head.

This wasn't a gentle kiss at all. It was desperate and rough, our mouths ravaging each other and quickly spiraling out of control. It felt like it had been forever since I was last able to touch him. Before long, I was gasping for air, trying to breathe him into me. To hold on to this moment and him forever.

38

"Sugar, we can't do this here," he whispered against my lips as my hands started to unbutton his shirt. I had forgotten we were in my parents' driveway. Forgotten that they were probably waiting for me inside the house.

"Shit," I replied, my head dropping down to his chest. I could feel his heart thumping under my cheek. His arms wrapped around me so he could cradle me in his embrace. I loved being this close to him. How could I ever give this up?

I felt his lips press against the top of my head . "Now that I've finally got you back home, I don't know want to let you go. Even knowing I get to see you tomorrow, it's taking everything I have inside me not to turn this truck on and steal you away for the night."

"Is it really stealing me away if I want to go with you?"

Shane squeezed me even tighter at my response. "Tonight it would be. Your parents are excited to have you home. Your dad lets me get away with a lot, but I'm pretty sure he'd be hunting me down if I took off with you tonight."

"I know you're right, but I need you so much."

"Fuck," he whispered. "You can't say shit like that right now, Char. I'm dying here. I need you, too. And knowing how much you want me is killing me."

"I'm sorry," I whimpered.

"Shhhh, sugar. You never have to apologize for that. It just goes against everything inside me to leave you wanting, but there isn't a damn thing I can do about it tonight."

"Who knew my being home would make it even harder for us to be together?"

"Fuck, you're brilliant! Go on into the house, but do not fall asleep. Say goodnight to your parents, head up to your room, and get ready for bed like you normally would do. But bring your laptop with you."

"My laptop?" I questioned.

"Oh, yeah. I never thought I would ever want to say these words again, but I think tonight calls for another Skype session. I can't take you here in my truck with your parents right inside, but I sure as hell won't leave you in need all night long," he swore.

My heart raced at his words as my body tingled with desire. "Hurry home," I urged as he redid the buttons I'd managed to undo before he slid out of the truck and lifted me down. He gave me a quick kiss and nudged me towards the house. I walked swiftly up the steps and waited for him to start the engine before going inside.

My parents must have trusted me to do the right thing more than they should have because it looked like they had already headed to bed. Thank God because talking to them right now was the last thing I wanted to do. I followed Shane's instructions and waited for him to text me that he'd made it back home safely. I had my Skype up and ready to go.

I waited a couple minutes so he could make it to his room and hit the call button. As soon as he picked up, I hit the video button and popped the call into full screen. Shane's face filled my view, and my nerves settled.

"Good girl," he said huskily before he leaned back and I saw that he'd already stripped out of his shirt and was lying on his bed with the top button of his dress pants undone.

"God, Shane. You are so fucking hot."

"Only for you, sugar. Now show me exactly how fucking hot I make you," he urged me.

I leaned against my pillows so he could see the pale green babydoll lingerie set I'd thrown on as I licked the tips of my fingers and trailed them down my neck. I could almost imagine his lips caressing me everywhere I touched as goose bumps prickled across my skin. My breasts felt heavy as I grasped one in each hand, squeezing through the fabric.

"Pull them out for me to see," he demanded, his voice thickened with need.

I pulled the straps off my shoulders and let the nightie drop so my breasts were exposed to his gaze through the screen. My nipples puckered in the air, begging for his touch. I plucked at them, rolling each nipple between two fingers and pinching lightly. It was incredibly arousing to hear Shane's growl as he watched my play with myself.

"Lower. Show me how much you miss me. How much you need me."

My fingers complied with his demands without any hesitation. I lifted up a little to shimmy out of the babydoll, and he growled when he saw that I hadn't bothered to put any panties on. My pussy glistened with the proof of my desire for him.

"So much, Shane. I need you so much," I murmured as I moved my fingers down my body. I couldn't wait much longer. I wanted to race to the finish line tonight. I held myself open with one hand so he could see

40

everything I was doing as I teased my clit, lightly pinching it. I could feel my walls clenching, desperate for the feel of Shane inside me, and my eyes drifted shut. I knew that wasn't going to happen tonight, so I reached blindly for the vibrator I had placed on the bed next to me.

"No, Char," Shane snapped. "This is the last time we are doing this over Skype, and I want you so much that I'm even jealous of your vibrator tonight. Use your fingers instead. I want to see you lick yourself off them when you're all done."

I dropped the vibrator back down on the bed and spread my legs a little bit wider before running my fingers up my thighs. I heard the sound of Shane undoing his zipper, and my eyes popped open so I wouldn't miss a thing. I knew I wasn't going to last very long. I was already on a razor-sharp edge. The slightest touch was bound to send me over.

I watched as his cock sprang free from his pants, thrilled to know that he had gone commando all day even while he had been all dressed up for me. I watched him grip his cock tight at the base and realized that he was right there on the edge with me, and I desperately wanted to push him over as fast as I possibly could. There wasn't anything hotter in this world than watching Shane as he came.

"Mmmmmm, I wish this was your cock," I murmured as I plunged two fingers inside my pussy.

"Fuck, so do I," Shane groaned as his hand stroked up and down.

"You'd be so deep inside me right now, filling me up and driving in and out."

His eyes clenched shut at my words as he tried to hold his climax back.

"Look at me, baby. Watch me while I pretend it's you inside me right now. I'm so close already. I want you so much."

His eyes flashed darkly as he opened them. "Come for me now," he demanded. "Now, Char."

I added another finger and slammed them inside, using my other hand to rub my clit. I heard Shane's groan and the sound of him so close sent me over the edge.

"Shane," I whimpered.

"So fucking beautiful," he murmured. "And all mine."

"Yours," I agreed.

"Feeling better?" he asked smugly, a cocky grin spreading across his gorgeous face.

"Yeah. I think I can make it until tomorrow now."

"Good girl. You come find me as soon as you're free, okay?"

"Mmmkay," I sighed.

"Go to sleep, Char. I'll see you tomorrow," I heard him say as I drifted off to sleep.

CHAPTER
Three

Shane

I WOKE UP REFRESHED this morning, more prepared to face the day than I had been in the last four years. Knowing that Charlotte was just across town at her parents' eased something inside me, a tension that had stayed with me while she'd been away at school. I'd never really wanted to admit to it, not even to myself, but there had been this fear within me that she wouldn't come home. That she would decide that there was more out there for her to explore and that I'd be left with a decision to make about what to do next. Deciding to wait for her while she went to school had been easy for me. It wasn't like there was anyone else I wanted to be with but Charlotte. But if she had decided that she wanted something other than life in my hometown, I wasn't sure what I would have done.

My plan had always been to work on my dad's farm with the horses and take over when he was ready to retire. It was the only thing I knew and I loved doing it. Plus, if I didn't stay here, then there wasn't anyone else who could work it when he was done. I was their only child, so it was me or nothing. I'd grown up fully expecting to raise my own children on this land, and the idea of the farm passing outside of the family after being ours for so many years was something I just didn't think I could accept. Not even for Charlotte.

Luckily, I didn't have to worry about that anymore. She was home, right where she belonged, and now we could plan our future together. Pretty soon I was going to be able to wake up with her in bed next to me. I didn't know how the hell I was ever going to get my morning chores done on time when that happened. Just the thought of having her here with me made my morning wood rock hard.

As I jumped out of bed to head to the shower, I thanked my lucky stars that my move to the apartment above the garage afforded me some privacy. I wasn't going to stay here forever since my dad had already deeded me some property to build on, but it sure came in handy at times like this when I knew there was no way in hell my cock was going to go down any time soon. Jacking off in the shower in my parents' house when I was a teenager was one thing. Doing it as a grown-ass man just wasn't right. Plus, I could sleep naked without worrying about my mom barging into my room in the mornings.

I flipped the shower on to get it nice and steamy while brushing my teeth. It had been a hectic couple of days with the trip down for Char's graduation. I figured I should probably squeeze in a shave if I was going to see her today, but I knew it made her even hotter when I had a bit of scruff. And seeing the marks it left behind on her skin drove me crazy. That was reason enough for me to skip shaving today.

I stepped into the shower and couldn't help the smile that crossed my face upon seeing Charlotte's favorite shower products in there. My mom was one hell of a smart woman. She must have grabbed them for me, knowing that I'd do everything I could to get her to move in with me this summer. I flipped open the cap on the body wash and breathed in the smell of cotton candy that always clung to Charlotte. It made me think of nibbling and biting her skin and leaving a trail behind that marked my possession of her body.

I squirted some of the body wash onto my hand before wrapping it around my hardened cock. The steam from the shower made the scent swirl around me, helping me picture Charlotte there with me—on her knees with her hair wrapped in my fists as I pummeled in and out of her mouth. She knew exactly how to torture me with blowjobs after so many years together.

I rested one hand on the shower wall for balance as my head dropped backwards. Eyes closed, I could picture her sucking me off so easily. My fist slipped up and down my shaft, her body wash making it slick. It was almost like her mouth would feel, making it even easier to imagine that it was her blowing me instead of my hand jacking me off.

I wanted to take my time and make it last, so I moved as slowly as I could. If she were here right now, her nipples would graze against my legs as she bobbed back and forth on my cock. I'd be able to hold myself still inside her mouth as she swirled her tongue over the slit in my cock to taste the pre-cum that I rubbed with my thumb.

Shit, it didn't matter how slow I went. I could already feel the telltale tingling in my balls and my feet started to clench on the tile floor. If I had wanted it to last, I shouldn't have pictured Charlotte's lips wrapped around my dick with her green eyes staring up at me with desire. Eyes filled with longing, knowing that as soon as I shot my load deep into her throat I'd return the favor by eating her pussy until I made her squirm.

And that last thought—the thought of the taste of her against my tongue—tossed my control out the window. My hips started pumping, driving my cock into my fist as I raced towards my climax. There was no thought of drawing this out anymore, just of completion as my balls drew tight against my body before my cock exploded against the shower wall. My chest heaved and my heart pounded, but I still wasn't fully satisfied. Not even after having watched her come for me last night. Nothing would take away this hunger that burned in me until I could get my girl under me over and over again. It had been too long since I had been able to sink deep inside her.

I finished up my shower as quickly as I could, spurred into action by the thought that the sooner I finished what needed to be done today, the sooner I could see Charlotte. As I headed out the door, I sent her a quick text giving her my schedule for the day and making sure she knew that she had better plan on being with me tonight. Because there was no way in hell I was taking no for an answer.

CHAPTER
Four

Charlotte

I SLEPT IN REALLY late, an unusual occurrence around our house. I figured my mama was giving me a couple of days to adjust to being home from school. How she managed to keep the rugrats out of my room, I had no idea.

I grabbed my phone off my nightstand and found a bossy text from Shane about how I should plan to spend my evening. I never thought I'd end up with someone so domineering. He was the exact opposite of my daddy, who pretty much let my mama get away with just about anything she wanted. She had him wrapped around her little finger, and I always figured that I'd end up with the same type of man in my life. Someone who catered to my every whim.

Not that I didn't know how to get what I wanted from Shane most of the time. Which was probably mostly due to the fact that we usually wanted the same things. Besides which, I found bossiness downright sexy on him. There was just something about knowing that I could trust him completely and hand over the reins that made me love him even more.

But today he was due for a surprise because there was no way in hell

I was willing to wait until the end of the day to see him. Not after our call last night. Sure, I'd been able to climax on my own with some help from him. But it just wasn't the same as having him inside me, and I'd waited long enough. So it was time to plan a sneak attack. Something he wouldn't see coming.

I glanced at the clock and did some quick calculations in my head. Odds were that I had just enough time to get ready, prepare a picnic, and head out to meet him when he was ready for lunch. Only it wouldn't be just food on the menu.

"WELL AREN'T YOU just a sight for sore eyes," Shane drawled out as I drove the Kawasaki Mule up to the pasture he was working in this morning.

I'd chosen to wear a green sundress today, one of his favorite colors on me. I had paired it with brown boots and pulled my hair into a braid that trailed down one side. I also hadn't worn any panties, which Shane was going to find out about before I left to go home.

"I certainly hope so," I teased as I twirled around in front of him.

"Pretty as can be," he replied before he wiped his brow with the red bandana he carried in his jeans pocket when he worked. The sun gleamed in his dark hair, and his shirt clung to his chest. Add in the stubble on his chin and he looked sexy as hell.

I stuck my ass out as I leaned into the Mule to grab the picnic basket and blanket. I could practically feel his eyes boring into me, just like I wanted.

"I brought you lunch," I said, handing him the basket. "Hope you don't mind if I stay though."

"Char, I never mind spending extra time with you. Ever," he murmured before leaning over to give me a kiss. "If you decided to bring me lunch every single damn day, I'd be the happiest guy in town."

My heart melted at his words. How could I not love this guy? Surely having him in my life was worth whatever crap I'd have to take from the local beauty queen brigade.

I laid the blanket out on the grass at the bottom of a hill, and Shane opened up the basket and started pulling out our lunch. I hadn't really packed anything special for us to eat, just sandwiches, chips, and cookies. Lunch was secondary to my main goal in coming out here, so I didn't really care what we ate.

We sat across from each other on the blanket and finished off the food pretty quickly. Shane was always hungry, especially when he was working outside. It felt nice to be the one to feed him.

As soon as we'd cleaned up the mess, I pulled him back down with me. "Can you stay for a little bit longer?"

"Sure," he murmured as he leaned back, pulling me with him.

I twisted in his arms so that I lay on top of his body. There wasn't a soul around. It was just the two of us out here all by ourselves. Perfect.

"Shane," I whispered before kissing his across his jaw and placing a gentle kiss on his mouth.

"Char," he whispered back, a smile tilting his lips in the corner. His eyes were closed as he enjoyed the quiet moment between us.

"I love you so much." I couldn't help the words that rushed out. My heart was bursting at the seams.

"It's a good thing, sugar. 'Cause I love you too and I've finally got you right where I want you."

My heart jolted at his response, a lump forming in my throat. I felt so incredibly guilty for not talking to him about my fears and second thoughts about moving back home. But no matter what the future brought, I wanted to enjoy this one perfect moment in time with Shane.

"I need you," I whispered against his lips, my hand moving down his body to cup his quickly hardening length.

He opened his eyes and looked at me, desire burning in their dark depths. "I always need you, Char."

I quickly unbuckled his belt, popped the button on his jeans, and pulled down the zipper. I'd been thinking about this moment since I woke up this morning, so I didn't hesitate as I grabbed the base of his cock and slid down its length. A look of shock crossed Shane's face before he clenched his jaw and groaned.

It had been so long since I'd felt him hard and hot inside me, stretching me bit by bit. I heaved a sigh as I savored the feel of Shane's cock deep in me.

"Fuck," he muttered in a raspy voice. His *fingers* curled into my hips as he guided me lower. "Tell me that feels as good for you as it does for me."

"I can't even begin to describe it," I gasped, rocking my hips down to bring him farther into me.

I wanted more of him, needed every single inch buried inside me. I lifted myself back up to repeat the action, but he grabbed my waist and pulled me down again.

"Need more," he rasped out as we start moving in rhythm. As quickly as I would lift my hips, his hands would lower me back down.

"Shane," I whimpered as he kissed me everywhere he could reach. Across my cheeks, down my neck, along my collarbone, and near the edge of my bodice. He nudged both straps off my shoulders so that my sundress gaped open, revealing my bare breasts.

"Mine," he growled before he licked my nipples. I felt his *fingers* digging into my skin as we began to move faster against each other. He laved each breast and softly bit into my skin, leaving a slight sting behind as he released it.

"Yours," I agreed, tangling my hands in his hair and pulling his head so that I could stare into his eyes as I moved.

"God, Charlotte! You're so fucking beautiful," he said in a sex-roughened voice that sent chills up my spine.

I leaned down to kiss him, needing the taste of him in my mouth as he took over our motions, rocking his hips up and pulling me down at the same time. I could feel the strength of his muscles underneath me as he controlled me even while I was in a supposed position of power.

"Harder. Please, Shane," I begged.

"Tell me you love me," he demanded.

"Shane," I whimpered.

He held his hips still for a moment. "Say it and I'll give you exactly what you want. What you need," he rasped.

"I love you," I moaned, rocking my hips, trying to keep him deep inside.

"That's my girl," he whispered before grabbing my hips harder and filling me completely. Giving me what I needed to send me over the edge.

Waves of pleasure poured over my body. "Shane!" I screamed.

"I love you, Char," I heard him murmur before he crushed his lips against mine. His mouth was demanding as he surged inside one last time before climaxing.

My body collapsed against his as though I had been drained of every last ounce of energy. A smile lit across my face as I listened to the sound of his heart beating wildly under my cheek. Moments like this were exactly why I needed to stay in town. I couldn't imagine ever feeling this close to anyone else in the entire world. Being with Shane had to be worth the moments of doubt I had about where I fit in in this tiny town.

"What time are you coming over to my place tonight?" he asked huskily. "I think I owe you something special after your little surprise."

"I'm not sure yet if I can make it over. It depends on how much help Daddy needs at the bar."

"Shit, Char. It's your first night back. Can't you take a little time off to enjoy being home?" he complained.

"I'll do my best to make it an early night," I promised, not knowing that the week was going to fly by with my helping out at the bar for my daddy and at home for my mama when three of my siblings came down with a bug all at the same time.

Shane

A WEEK GOING BY with hardly being able to see Charlotte after she'd finally come back home was something I could barely tolerate. I understood that she had family obligations, but I wanted her first responsibility to be to me. And there was only one way to make that happen. I needed to make her my wife.

My parents had known for months that I planned to ask Charlotte to marry me. I'd worked with my dad to pick out the land where I would build our home. My mom had gone with me to the jewelry store to help me pick out a ring. But I hadn't talked to Char's father yet, and I needed to ask for his permission before I could pop the question. He wasn't the type of man who would take my asking her without first approaching him very lightly. So I had called him to ask if I could meet up with him while Charlotte was watching over the bar tonight.

I didn't think I had been this nervous since my first date with her when I arrived at her home to find him waiting on the porch, sitting in a rocking chair with a shotgun sitting across his lap. He'd told me that they hadn't lived in town long enough to have heard any good things about me, but he hadn't heard anything bad either. That he was trusting me with his baby girl, and he fully expected me to honor that trust. When he asked me back then if I was going to treat Charlotte with respect, I'd answered him honestly when I said yes.

She'd earned that respect by making me work to get her to agree to a dinner date in the first place. I remembered thinking that if any other girl's father had asked me the same question I would have been lying if I had given the same answer. I wasn't about to do anything now to show him less respect today than I had back then.

I waited until I knew Charlotte would be at the bar and everyone would be settling down before I headed over to her house. I didn't want her brothers or sisters to overhear our conversation because they would be bound to spoil the surprise for her. I needed to get in, talk to her dad, and get out before anyone realized I was there. Luckily, it seemed that he had a similar idea because I once again found him waiting on the porch for me.

This time, there wasn't a shotgun on his lap but a Benjamin Prichard's Double Barreled Bourbon instead. Charlotte's dad was a Tennessee whiskey man and this was one of his favorite bottles. So either he had figured out why I wanted to see him and was ready to give me his blessing or he was just getting ready to drink me under the table. Figuratively of course, because there wasn't a table to be seen, just the two rocking chairs, the bottle on his lap and two glasses sitting at his feet.

"Shane? You gonna come on up here and join me or stand there waiting all night?" he asked.

I wiped my sweaty palms on my jeans and walked up the steps. "I'm going to join you of course."

"About damn time," he muttered. "I've been waiting to crack this bottle open. Grab the glass for me, will you?"

I reached down and held them out so he could pour the amber liquid into both glasses. A whiff of oaky booze drifted towards my nose, making my mouth water a little. I wasn't a huge fan myself, but there was no way in hell I was going to turn the man down right now.

I took a small sip and the liquid burned down my throat, leaving a taste of oak and vanilla in its wake. I coughed a little, making Charlotte's dad laugh loudly.

"That'll put hair on a man's chest, won't it, son?"

"Yeah," I rasped out in agreement and dropped down into the chair next to him.

"So what brings you over tonight?" he asked, getting right to the point as he was apt to do. Charlotte's dad wasn't one to beat around the bush.

"Well," I started before clearing my throat, "I wanted to talk to you about Charlotte's and my future."

"Okay. You've got my attention," he said as he turned to look at me with a serious expression on his face.

"You know that I love your daughter," I continued.

"Yes, you've shown us how much she means to you by letting Charlotte go pursue our dream for her and staying with her even when it wasn't easy to do," he agreed. "Not a lot of boys your age would've made the same decision."

"Here's the thing. She's the one for me. I've known it practically since we met. I might not have understood it back then, but I certainly do now. And I want to spend the rest of my life with her, sir."

"Can't say that it surprises me to hear you say that," he replied. "So what are you going to do about it?"

Shit. I realized I hadn't even managed to get my question out. "I'd like to ask you for her hand in marriage, sir. I want to ask Charlotte to be my wife."

"And do you think she's ready to get married, son? That she's going to say yes if you ask her?" he wanted to know.

"I hope so, but I guess I won't know for sure until the time comes for her to answer me. What do you think?"

"I think none of us are really ready to get married until we find ourselves tied to the one person we love more than anyone else. It's hard work, but I know neither of you is afraid of that. You've proven that you're willing to work to keep her in your life. And I've watched my baby girl around you. Her whole face lights up any time you're near. I could certainly do a whole lot worse when it comes to a son-in-law."

"Does that mean I have your permission to ask her?" I asked.

"Yes, Shane. You have my permission to marry my daughter as long as that's what she wants."

I heaved a deep sigh, a feeling of relief washing over me. "Thank you, sir."

"You're welcome, son. Now you better drink up. You look like you could use it," he said as he gestured to my almost full glass.

I took a big gulp of the liquid. Then my eyes started to water and my throat began to feel like it was on fire. "Jesus," I swore. "How can you drink this stuff?"

"We'll make a bourbon drinker out of you yet," he joked. "Now that I've got years to do it. Although maybe I should try something a little milder next time."

CHAPTER
Six

Charlotte

I WASN'T REALLY IN the mood tonight to be in charge of the bar, but I hadn't felt like I could say no when my dad asked me. The last week had been rough on all of us, and my mama could really use his help around the house. Besides, being here was a hell of a lot better than being around all my sick siblings. The house felt like a hospital with all their coughing and the smell of medicine and bleach in the air. And the last thing I needed was to catch it now that everyone was finally starting to feel better.

Luckily, it was a crazy busy night, so time was flying by. It was a good thing since I was so tired. I hadn't been sleeping well since I kept dreaming that Shane and I got into a huge fight about me staying in town. I only hoped that it wasn't an omen of what was to come when we had the time to sit down and have a serious conversation.

I was pretty sure it was my guilty conscience sneaking up on me for not saying anything to him yet. But I was starting to feel hopeful that it wouldn't even be necessary since things had been going well since I had gotten home. Well, things around town that is. My mom had needed a lot of help, and it had given me the chance to see a lot of people while running errands for her. So far, everyone I had met again had been so nice and welcoming. A lot of the townspeople had congratulated me on my graduation and told me how happy they were that I was back to help my parents.

It seemed that my family had progress on being accepted while I was away. Either I hadn't noticed it during my summer breaks before or the same courtesies hadn't been extended to me until people had realized I was home from school for good. I probably shouldn't be surprised though. My mama was involved in just about everything around town between school activities, sports for the boys, owning the bar, and church. She was busy as hell and had a hard time saying no to people when they needed help with something.

Things at the bar were going well too. My dad had brought in a stage so that we could feature local performers, although there weren't too many who were that good from what my parents had told me. But people seemed to appreciate the chance to sing in front of an audience and it brought in the crowds, especially when he opened it up for karaoke Fridays. Unfortunately, that meant I got to listen to some of the worst sounds of my life tonight. And it had pulled in the beauty queen brigade—the girls who had given me such a hard time back in high school.

Suzanna, the queen bee and bane of my existence my senior year, had strolled into the bar a couple of hours ago like she owned the place. It amazed me that four years had passed and she looked practically identical to how she had back in high school—same big blond hair, way too much makeup, and clothes that looked to me a couple of sizes too small for her. You would have thought with how strict her parents were that she'd dress more appropriately, but she'd always managed to wrap them around her finger so they'd overlook how slutty she looked. And acted.

That girl hated me so much back in school. She never let me forget that I was the new girl in town and that I didn't fit in. That there was no place for me here. And it looked like her feelings on the subject hadn't changed much in four years either with the haughty look she'd given me as she and her friends had picked a table. I'd sent a waitress over because there was no way in hell I was going to serve her myself. I didn't think I would be able to manage it without tossing a drink in her face instead.

I always knew the reason she hated me so much was that she wanted Shane for herself. She had made no secret of the fact back in the day. She

56

flirted with him any time she saw him, regardless of if she had a boyfriend at the time or that he had me in his life. I wasn't exactly sure why she thought he belonged with her since she wasn't one of his conquests from before me. They had known each other forever since they were neighbors, so if Shane had wanted to go there, he certainly could have way before he met me.

Shane had mentioned that Suzanna was starting to come around more often lately too. He was totally clueless to the fact that she was doing it to try to take him away from me. He didn't see her that way at all and thought of her as the annoying neighbor girl he had played with as a little boy. When I had told him that it bothered me, he swore that she was harmless even though she was a little bit bitchy and that he'd talk to her about it. She'd always been very careful to never be too catty to me when he was around because she knew that he wouldn't let her get away with it.

Shane figured I was just feeling a little bit jealous, and he had the nerve to tell me that he liked it. That it made him hot to think that I wanted him so much that I didn't want him hanging out with a childhood friend. I'd never made a big deal out of my issues with her, so it was hard to explain to him why she pissed me off so much and why I didn't trust her around him. Which was okay because I was able to turn the tables on him when I asked him how he'd feel if I decided to hang out with one of my old friends from before I moved to town—who happened to be a boy. That had shut him up real fast because there was no way he would be cool with me hanging out with other guys, even if it was innocent.

And now here she was, in my bar, acting like she owned the place. She'd sent her drink back twice, saying that they hadn't been made right. Her waitress was just about in tears from the bullshit she had put her through so far and it had only been a couple of hours. I would have been well within my rights to tell her to leave. I didn't have to serve anyone I didn't want to, but I really didn't want to start a war with Suzanna. Not if I was going to make my home here. But she sure was reminding me of all my doubts about staying. Did I really want to put up with this kind of crap for the rest of my life? Could I even manage to do it if I decided I wanted to? For Shane?

As those thoughts rolled through my mind, Suzanna decided that she'd had enough of my ignoring her so she came to me instead. "Well if it isn't little Miss Carrot Top herself," she slurred.

My hair might be red, but it certainly didn't resemble a carrot, so I let the insult pass this time. Back in high school, I would have reacted, but living with Kaylie had taught me to hold my tongue every once in a while.

"Suzanna," I replied.

"What the hell do you think you're doing?" she asked.

I looked down around the bar for a moment, not exactly sure what she was getting at since it was clear that I was working. It wasn't like she didn't know that my parents owned the place, after all.

"Working," I answered.

"No," she carried on, waving her arms around. "I'm not talking about what you're doing here tonight. I know that you're working. I'm not dumb."

She stopped to look at me like I should agree with her, which was hard to do since I really didn't think she was the brightest bulb in the pack. So I just nodded my head. It seemed to be enough of a response for her though.

"I mean what the hell are you doing back here?"

I took a moment to really think about her question before responding. "Well, Suzanna, I do live here."

"But you don't belong around here," she argued. "You hightailed it right out of town as fast as you could to go to college. You knew in high school that you didn't fit in here, so why have you come back now?"

"Shane's here," I said simply, knowing it would taunt her since, at the bottom of it all, this was really about him. That I had him when she wanted him for herself.

The bar had quieted down as everyone's attention turned to our confrontation. "Of course Shane's here. He'll always be here. This is where he grew up, right on the farm next to mine. But that doesn't mean you have to stay too."

"He's my boyfriend, Suzanna. As much as you might hate it, the bottom line is he chose me. He loves me. And he stayed with me even when I went away for school."

"Huh," she snorted. "He was fine while you were away at school and he'd be fine if you left for good. Maybe then he'd be able to find someone who could make him happier than you ever could. Someone who understands what he wants out of life and can help him."

At that, my temper snapped. "Oh really, Suzanna? And who do you think that would be? You?"

"Yes!" she screamed. "If it hadn't been for you coming into town and taking him away, he would have been mine anyway. It was always meant to be Shane and me together until you messed it all up."

I couldn't help the laugh that bubbled up at her answer because she was flat-out delusional if that's what she thought. "Hell no, Suzanna. You're batshit crazy if you ever thought that you'd end up with Shane. He doesn't see you like that. He's never seen you like that. And he never will."

"Argh!" she shrieked, wagging her finger at me. "Yes he would if you would just do the right thing and leave for good! I've seen the way he looks at me sometimes when we're hanging out while you've been away. He would too want me if you weren't in the picture."

A sense of calm hit me as I finally realized that it didn't matter where I lived. Shane was mine. He was my home, and there was no way in hell I was going to let a jealous bitch rule my life and run me out of town, away from the man I loved. Away from my family. I'd been crazy to even think about it in the first place. Shane was it for me, and I was the only one for him. This was our home, and I was here to stay.

"No, Suzanna. He wouldn't want you if I was gone because he loves me. And you're nothing like me. I don't know what crazy daydream you've built up in your head about Shane, but it's about damn time for you to let it go. Because he's never going to be yours. He's mine for good and I'm here to stay."

Katherine, one of her friends came up to pull her away from me. "Suzanna, stop. You're causing a scene."

"I don't care! It isn't right that she's with Shane. He's too good for her, and I'm going to be stuck having to pick a nobody like Billy Joe."

At that, Katherine dropped her hands and stopped trying to help. "Billy Joe? My Billy Joe?"

"Bah," Suzanna shrugged her off. "He hasn't been yours in years."

"Shit, Suzanna. You really are a bitch. I can't believe you'd even consider dating your best friend's nobody of an ex-boyfriend. The one you told me to dump in the first place. And to think I've stood behind you all these years and listened to the trash you've spewed about Charlotte and how she stole Shane right out from under you," she said before turning to me. "I'm sorry. A lot of us were really mean to you back then because she had convinced us all that you were a horrible person. Looks like we were wrong."

I was stunned by the sudden turn of events as several people in the bar were giving Suzanna dirty looks. The rest of her friends were gathering up their stuff and throwing some cash on the table.

I accepted her apology. "Thank you."

"If you know what's good for you, you'll keep her as far from Shane as you possibly can. She's toxic," the girl finished before walking out of the bar with the rest of her friends.

Suzanna had a blank look on her face, like she couldn't believe what had just happened.

"I think you'd better go too, don't you, Suzanna? And maybe it would be best if you didn't come back to the bar again."

"But—" she sputtered.

"And I will be having a conversation with Shane about all the shit you've pulled over the years. So don't be surprised when he decides to drop your ass. The only reason he was still your friend was because I never said a word. But that time has passed, and when it comes down to it, anyone who knows Shane knows he's going to do what's best for me any day of the week."

The remaining customers hooted and hollered in agreement at my words. Suzanna's face turned beet red as she finally realized that she'd completely lost it in front of an audience. She stomped out, and I felt lighter than I had in years. I'd finally done what I should have done years ago—I had confronted the cause of most of my problems in town and walked away the winner.

CHAPTER
Seven

Shane

WORD SPREAD LIKE wildfire through town about Charlotte's confrontation with Suzanna. I'd heard about it first thing this morning and was a little pissed that she hadn't mentioned it to me herself when we spoke on the phone last night. Yeah, I got that it was a short call because she'd been really tired by the time she'd gotten home and my mind had been on my conversation with her dad. But I didn't like having to hear from someone else that a girl I'd known forever had been a total bitch to my girlfriend.

Part of loving her meant that it was my job to protect Charlotte. And I didn't feel like I had done a very good job of that if what I'd heard was true. It made me sick to know that I'd allowed Suzanna to be a part of my life while she was hurting Char.

I was utterly furious with myself for not seeing it sooner. The little comments here and there that had been meant to undermine my relationship, to make me doubt Char's love for me at a time when a true friend would have provided support knowing how hard the long-distance relationship had been on both of us. I had always figured it was because she didn't get it since she'd never fallen in love the way I had with Char.

It turned out that all this time she had been doing it on purpose, hoping to split us up. God only knows what shit she'd pulled with Charlotte over the years. And that's what burned me up the most—knowing that my girl had suffered because I hadn't seen the truth sitting right in front of me.

No more, I swore to myself. Now that I knew about it, I was going to take care of the Suzanna situation once and for all so we could move on to the future I had planned for us without any dark clouds hanging over our heads.

I hightailed it over to their farm next door and pounded on the front door. I hadn't called first, and I usually didn't just stop by first thing in the morning. I knew it might piss her daddy off, but I didn't think even they would appreciate the stunt she'd pulled last night since she'd managed to alienate most of the town. There had already been whispers about her dating history, and this was just the icing on the cake.

"Shane, is everything all right?" Suzanna's father asked as he opened the door, a worried expression on his face.

I hated to be disrespectful to a man who'd known me since the day I was born, but I needed him to know that I meant business too. "No, sir. I'm sorry to bother you so early in the morning, but I need to speak to your daughter. Now."

My tone of voice got his dander up a bit, but he still called Suzanna to the door. She looked surprised to see me but happy that I had come calling. She clearly didn't recognize the look of anger I was sure was spread across my face, totally clueless to what was going on around her.

When she stepped outside, her father joined us with his arms crossed in front of his body. He knew this wasn't going to be good, and I understood that, as her father, he wanted to be there to protect Suzanna. But that didn't mean I was going to spare her a shred of my anger.

"Suzanna, I heard about what happened last night, and I cannot believe you would be so horrible to Charlotte like that," I began.

Suzanna reached out to grab my arm, but I yanked away from her, making it clear how mad I was. "But, Shane, you've only heard her side of the story. It isn't fair for you to judge until I've had a chance to tell you what happened too," she complained. "Although I'm not surprised she ran straight to you to tell tales about me. She's never liked our friendship."

"That's where you're wrong. Charlotte didn't come to me about this.

I've had five different phone calls this morning from people around town, some of whom are supposed to be your closest friends. And yet she hasn't said a single word to me about it. She's never complained once about anything you've said or done, respecting the fact that we were childhood friends. But you can't say the same, can you?"

"Whatever do you mean?" she asked innocently.

"All these years, I never realized that you hated her so much. That you could be so spiteful and mean to someone I loved. What happened to the little girl I grew up with? How in the hell could you have turned into the type of person that would try to destroy something that makes me so happy?"

"Suzanna, honey, what on earth did you do last night?" her daddy asked.

A frustrated look crossed her face as Suzanna realized there was no getting out of this. Not only was I pissed at her, but her parents were going to hear about the whole thing too. Not just from me either.

"I just tried to make Charlotte see reason is all."

"And by reason, you mean you told her she didn't belong in this town and she didn't deserve to have me in her life? What the hell were you thinking?"

"Argh!" she growled before stomping her foot. "I was thinking exactly what I said. Maybe I shouldn't have done it, but dammit, Shane! It's supposed to be me and you! Ever since we were kids, it was supposed to be me that you picked! But you never did, and then she came to town and you were a lost cause. Totally blind to the fact that she's horribly wrong for you."

"Oh, Suzanna," her father sighed, shaking his head.

"No, Daddy! You've always seen it too! I've lost track of how many times you've said how perfect it would be for us to combine the two farms. How wonderful Shane is. I know how much you wished he was your son, and he could be if he would just open his eyes, stop thinking with his dick, and see how perfect we would be together!"

"That's enough out of you, missy. Go inside now. We'll talk about this later," he said, pointing at the door.

I'd never heard him use that tone of voice with Suzanna in all the years I'd known him. He'd always treated her like his princess, but look how that had turned out. She looked at me longingly as she walked through the door.

"Shane, son. I'm terribly sorry for the trouble my daughter has caused. You have my word that it won't happen again. And she will call Charlotte and apologize for her behavior."

"I'd appreciate that, sir. But I hope you understand when I say that she isn't welcome on my land anymore. It isn't just going to be my home from now on. It's going to be Charlotte's too, and there is no way I'm going to let anyone make her feel like she doesn't belong there beside me. No matter how long I've known them. Not when I plan to make her my wife."

"I hate that it's come to this, but I hear what you're saying. I hope sometime in the future y'all will be able to move past my daughter's actions," he said.

"That will be up to Charlotte, sir. If she ever decides she's ready to forgive Suzanna and wants her in our life, then that's when we'll move past this. I'm sorry, but until then, I'm done."

He shook his head sadly. "You've turned into one hell of a man, Shane. Your Charlotte is a lucky woman."

"That's just it, sir. I'm the lucky one. She's helped make me the man I am today," I said before walking away.

CHAPTER
Eight

Charlotte

SHANE DIDN'T SOUND happy when he called me to tell me he was on his way over. My head was still fuzzy from sleep since I hadn't gotten to bed until very late, so I didn't even think of a response before he hung up. I hated when he was pissed about something, and after the scene from last night I didn't really have the energy to argue with him about whatever was going on.

I pulled on some clothes and wandered downstairs only to find the house was completely silent. Mama had said she and Daddy might take everyone out for breakfast this morning so that I could sleep in now that the plague seemed to be over. It was a shame that Shane had woken me up instead.

There was a pot of coffee made, a covered pot on the stove and a note with my name on it on the kitchen counter. I flipped it open to see that my mama had made my favorite breakfast before they all left. There was nothing like cheesy grits to get your day started.

I spooned out a bowl and enjoyed each savory bite while I was waiting for Shane to arrive. It was nice to have a moment of peace and quiet, even if I knew that Shane was going to barge in any minute now to talk about whatever burr he had up his bonnet. I snorted a little at that thought, right before I heard a quick rap on the door and the sound of it opening.

"I'm back here," I yelled out to Shane so he could find me at the kitchen table.

He didn't say a word as he walked over and lifted me to my feet and wrapped me into a big ole' bear of a hug. We stood together for a few moments, Shane practically squeezing me to death.

I was worried it was something really bad with the way he was acting. "Hey, what happened?" I asked, my voice muffled by his shirt.

"Why didn't you ever say anything?" he asked.

That wasn't what I expected him to say at all. "About what?" I wondered aloud.

"Charlotte, how am I supposed to be able to protect you from harm when you won't even tell me how badly someone has been treating you?"

Aha, the light bulb went off in my head. Someone had gotten to Shane this morning before he and I had talked about what happened at the bar with Suzanna last night.

"Up until last night it wasn't that big of a deal. She wasn't always very nice to me, but it wasn't like she was horrible," I tried to explain. "And you've known her since forever. I didn't want to ruin your friendship with her just because we didn't like each other."

"Yeah, it sucks to lose a friend, but that pales in comparison to the thought of losing you. I don't have time for anyone in my life who doesn't want to support our relationship. And certainly not for someone who wants to mess things up between us," he swore as he pulled away to look deeply into my eyes. "You're the most important person in my life, Charlotte. If someone is giving you a hard time, I need to know about it. Okay?"

He certainly had a point when he put it that way. "Yes, I understand. I probably should have talked to you about her sooner. And I definitely was going to talk to you today after what happened last night," I started as I proceeded to explain everything that had gone down with her the night before.

Shane listened to my explanation and then shared with me his conversation with her this morning. I was in awe of the fact that he'd gone barging next door to confront her, in front of her father no less. "So don't you worry about having to deal with her any more. I made it perfectly clear that she wasn't welcome around any longer.

"Shane, you can't tell your neighbor that she's not allowed at your parents' house. They might get angry with you for that since they've known her longer than me," I argued.

"No, sugar, they will both understand why I said what I did. Besides, that's not exactly what I said."

"I don't understand," I said, not following what he meant.

Shane ran a hand through his dark locks and looked up at the ceiling. "I need to show you instead of tell you," he said as he held his hand out to me. "Take a ride with me?"

"Of course," I said as I followed him out the door and into his red pickup truck.

We drove straight out to the farm, but Shane turned down a dirt path instead of heading over to the house. After a couple minutes he parked in the middle of a field, hopped out of the truck and grabbed a blanket from the back. I followed him, not sure why we were here, but willing to go along to see what he had planned.

When I moved to sit down on the blanket after he'd spread it in the grass he stopped me. "No, Charlotte. I need you standing up for this," he said before he stuck his hand into the front pocket of his jeans. I figured he was just putting his keys in there or something so I was shocked when he pulled a ring box out and got down on one knee.

"Ohmigod," I whispered as tears welled in my eyes.

Shane opened the box and held it up so I could see the diamond ring twinkling inside. "Charlotte," he sighed before taking a deep breath. "I know our relationship hasn't always been the easiest, but I hope you know how much I love you. I want the chance to show you exactly how much every single day for the rest of our lives."

"Shane," I whispered, tears dripping down my cheeks.

"Will you marry me, sugar? Be my wife? And the mother of my children? Build a home with me here on my family's farm, right where we are standing? Be the woman I will love with my dying breath?"

I nodded my head wildly in response to his question, swallowing the lump in my throat so I could answer. "Yes," I croaked out.

Shane had a huge grin on his face as he teased me. "I'm sorry. I couldn't quite catch your answer there. Was that a yes?"

"Yes, Shane," I answered as I looked around at the land surrounding us. "I want to be your wife. To be the mother of your children. And I'd love to build our home right here where you asked me to marry you."

"Hot damn!" he crowed before he slid the ring onto my finger. Then he swooped me up into his arms and twirled me around.

I giggled at his excitement and held my hand up so I could admire the look of his ring on my finger. It was a perfect fit, just like us. "Holy shit, Shane! We're going to get married."

"Hell yes we are! Just as soon as I can get you to walk down that aisle to me. I don't want to wait a minute longer than I have to. I want to make you my wife as soon as I possibly can."

"You do realize that if we rush it people will think this is a shotgun wedding, right?" I teased.

"If that's what it takes to get this done quickly, that's fine with me. You just tell your daddy to bring his gun, and I'll do my best to knock you up," he promised as he laid me down on the blanket.

I watched as he started to strip out of his clothes. "Right here?"

He nodded at me as he pulled his boots off. "Definitely here. We can christen our land the right way."

"Right now?" I asked

"No time like the present now that you're finally my fiancé," he said before he pounced and my clothes were tossed aside like he was a man on a mission to get me naked. Something I was more than happy to help him accomplish.

"Sounds like a good plan to me," I whispered as he leaned over me. Shane traced a fingertip down my cheek, with such a look of love on his face. "Since I need you."

"Charlotte, I will always give you anything you need. You know that," he swore.

I reached up to grab his thick, dark hair and pulled his head down towards mine. My lips met his, hungrily. I was suddenly desperate for his touch. I licked at his lips and sucked his tongue into my mouth, mimicking what I wanted him to do to me.

Shane lowered his body down onto mine, his hard flesh meeting my naked skin, warming me. He slid a hand down my body and parted my legs, trailing a finger up to the center of my need and sliding inside. I pushed against him, wanting to go fast. I needed him hard inside of me.

I tried to urge him closer, but Shane was too strong. "Please," I begged.

"Soon," he promised. "I need to make sure you're ready for me first."

He kissed me deep and long as he thrust a second finger into me and stretched me. But it still wasn't enough.

"Shane," I whimpered against his lips.

"Shhhh, I've got you," he replied as he trailed his mouth down my neck, licking the sensitive flesh at my throat while his fingers kept stroking me.

I arched toward him as the desire continued to build inside me, wrapping my legs around his hips and urging him towards my core.

"Now," I pleaded with him.

"Yes," he hissed. "Now."

Shane positioned his body and drove deep into me, his dark eyes locked on mine. I stared into them as he thrust over and over again, moving harder each time. I lost track of time. I couldn't hold a single thought in my head. I could only feel his body meeting mine, us moving together thrust for thrust.

Sweat glistened on his body, and I could feel the breeze against my slickened skin. But I couldn't look away from him. There was something so different about this time. A bigger connection between the two of us. One that I didn't want to break by looking away.

Shane locked his hands around my hips and lifted me up to meet his thrusts. He held me so easily, and I felt safe in his arms. Loved and cherished. Desired and ravished.

I felt my muscles start to tighten as I drew closer and closer to release. "So close," I whispered to him.

"God, me too, Charlotte. I don't know if I can hold on much longer," Shane growled.

Pleasure exploded at his words and rocked my body. I shuddered in his arms as my climax hit me, setting Shane off as he stiffened against me. I could feel the heat of his release filling me inside. He still kept pumping in and out as I shivered beneath him, aftershocks bursting over me and taking my breath away.

"So good," I murmured.

Shane leaned down and captured my lips with his before slowly withdrawing from my body. "Perfect," he replied.

We just laid there, tangled together for quite a while, enjoying the sense of closeness.

"You said yes," he whispered into my ear, rubbing the ring that circled my finger.

"I did," I replied.

"And pretty soon you'll say I do," he continued.

"Yes, I will."

"Mine," he whispered as he held my body close to his. And I was relieved that I no longer had any doubts about our future together.

EPILOGUE

Shane

THE DAY HAD finally come when I get to make Charlotte my wife. The sun was beaming down on me as I waited for the wedding march to begin. I tugged at my collar, not entirely comfortable wearing a tux even if it was my wedding day. It didn't help that I was feeling a little jittery since I'd hardly seen Charlotte all weekend. Her girlfriends came into town for the wedding and Kaylie had insisted that they had to do a bachelorette party even though Charlotte swore she didn't want or need one. Kaylie pretty much kidnapped her to make it happen, and then they all slept in late on Saturday. I didn't get to see her again until the rehearsal dinner, where afterwards her mom had taken the whole no seeing the bride thing way too seriously and swept Charlotte away for the rest of the night.

Glancing around, I was happy to see so many of our family and friends had joined us today. When Charlotte had said she wanted the wedding to be here in the field where I had proposed - where we were going to build our home and raise our family - I had to admit that I was a little skeptical that she'd be able to pull it off. Boy did she enjoy proving me wrong.

I was standing under a gazebo decorated with a wild array of flowers. Charlotte had always wanted one, so her dad surprised us by having it built for the wedding. Our guests were seated in rows of white chairs with a deep green runner down the center aisle just waiting for Charlotte to march towards me. A huge white tent stood off to the side for the reception that would follow the ceremony, with a giant dance floor in the middle of all the tables.

As the music changed, my attention swung towards the end of the aisle. I watched as Charlotte's youngest sister tossed flower petals on the ground and as each of her bridesmaids walked towards me, arm in arm with one of my groomsmen. And finally the moment came when Charlotte and her dad moved slowly towards me. She was drop dead gorgeous in her wedding dress, her tits looked like they might pop out at any minute, and each step revealed feet wrapped in fuck-me heels with straps criss-crossed around her ankles. Her pretty red curls were pulled away from her face and her lips begged to be kissed with red lipstick marking them.

"Shane," she whispered, smiling up at me as her father placed her hand in mine. Everything else faded into the background as I gazed into her green eyes and gripped her hand in mine.

"You ready to become my wife, sugar?" I asked in a teasing tone, hoping to get a little smile out of her as I watched tears well in her eyes. Her emotions have been all over the place lately with all the stress from planning the wedding.

"Absolutely!" she sighed as she flashed a smile at me and we turned so the ceremony tying us together for life could begin.

"YOU'VE GOT TO eat something," I whispered to Charlotte as I watched her sliding food across her plate during the reception. So far, she'd barely touched anything except for a few nibbles of bread and a couple sips of champagne and they were already clearing the plates.

"I will. I promise," she replied with a tilt to her lips as though she found my concern funny.

"Don't think for a second that I haven't noticed you've lost weight. I let it slide because I knew how focused you were on making today special, but that ends here and now. You're my wife, and it's my job to take care of you," I reminded her, lifting a bite to her mouth.

"Just you wait," she muttered under her breath before closing her lips over the fork.

"Wait for what?" I asked, confused when she just pointed at her mouth like she couldn't answer me since she was eating. And then she gestured at the stage where the band was trying to get everyone's attention so we could kick off the dancing with our first dance as a married couple.

"I'll let it drop for now, but you will eat something tonight even if I have to shove cake down your throat instead of mashing it into your face later," I warned her while I led her to the dance floor as they began to play "I Cross My Heart" by George Strait.

It was the song Charlotte's parents had danced to at their wedding and she'd insisted that it had to be ours too. I didn't have the heart to tell her no since it meant so much, but I did have a little surprise in store for her as well. When the song died down and she stepped away from me, there were tears rolling down her cheeks.

"Thank you," she whispered.

I pulled her close again as the band announced that the groom had a special request before they began to play "I Could Not Ask for More" by Sara Evans. The song meant everything to me because while we were dancing to it at our senior prom Charlotte had finally told me she loved me. I couldn't let tonight pass by without dancing with her again while this song played knowing she was now my wife.

I whispered along in her ear, and as I told her that I couldn't ask for more, Charlotte took my hand from her waist and placed it over her stomach. "You might not have to ask for more, but I'm going to give it to you anyway. You're going to be a daddy in about seven months, Shane."

I stopped abruptly as her words sunk in. "A daddy?" I asked in a whisper, almost afraid to hear her response and find out that I imagined it.

"I wanted to wait and tell you later tonight when we were alone, but I just couldn't hold out any longer. I know you had no idea when you planned this dance, but you gave me the perfect moment to share my news with you."

Everything suddenly clicked into place. The mood swings and weight loss weren't from planning our wedding. She wasn't drinking anymore because she was carrying my baby. "And you're okay with this?" I asked, worried that it was too soon for her.

"I'm better than okay, Shane," she said, squeezing my hand.

"Shit, I better get moving on our house then," I realized. As she giggled in response, I picked Charlotte up and twirled her around as I shouted at the top of my lungs, "We're having a baby!"

COMING SOON

Outside the BOX

BLYTHE COLLEGE 3

Aubrey earned her love 'em and leave 'em reputation with her serial dating past. A pregnancy scare makes her see the light and change her ways. She gets serious about school and stops dating – until she meets Luka and falls head over heels for him.

Luka doesn't trust easily after having his heart crushed by the girl next door. When he meets Aubrey, he doesn't think she's serious relationship material because of her past – even though he's drawn to her.

What happens when the girl who always ran the moment a relationship got serious meets *The One*? Will Aubrey be able to get Luka to see her *Outside the Box* he's put her in?

Acknowledgments

My Boys – I love you!!! Thanks for letting me get lost in my head sometimes when I'm in the middle of writing.

Mom – Thank you for always believing in me and pushing me to make this happen. I love you!

Mickey – I am so grateful to have found an editor like you! Thanks for putting your mad editing skills to good use for me.

Melissa – You did an amazing job with this cover. Thank you!

Yolanda – You've always been there for me, and your friendship means the world to me. Thanks for being my number one cheerleader!

Midian – Seriously, I don't know if there are words to describe what your input means to me. Thank you for being gentle while giving me your insight on how to make this a better story and kicking my butt when needed.

Love Between The Sheets Promotions & all the Bloggers who have supported me – Thanks for helping me get the word out about my books. The time you give to the reading world is very much appreciated.

Readers – Thanks for taking a chance on me! I hope you've enjoyed reading my stories as much as I've enjoyed writing them.

About the Author

I absolutely adore reading - always have and always will. My friends growing up used to tease me when I would trail after them, trying to read and walk at the same time. If I have downtime, odds are you will find me reading or writing.

I am the mother of two wonderful sons who have inspired me to chase my dream of being an author. I want them to learn from me that you can live your dream as long as you are willing to work for it.

When I told my mom that my new year's resolution was to self-publish a book in 2013, she pretty much told me "About time!"

Connect with me online!

Facebook: http://www.facebook.com/rochellepaigeauthor

Twitter: @rochellepaige1

Goodreads: https://www.goodreads.com/author/show/7328358.Rochelle_ Paige

Website: http://www.rochellepaige.com